MR. RILEY

English

BOBBY CINEMA

authorHOUSE®

AuthorHouse™
1663 Liberty Drive
Bloomington, IN 47403
www.authorhouse.com
Phone: 1 (800) 839-8640

Published by AuthorHouse 04/21/2015

ISBN: 978-1-5049-0846-7 (sc)
ISBN: 978-1-5049-0845-0 (e)

Print information available on the last page.

DEDICATED TO ADAM RICHARD
SANDLER AND TO HAPPY MADISON
PRODUCTIONS AND ALSO DEDICATED
TO HIS FAVORITE BASEBALL
TEAM NEW YORK YANKEES

Synopsis: A new sports movie with a new twist about a baseball team the The Runaway Boys, that is a screwball comedy about the trials and tribulations about an computer billionaire whiz kid Ryan Green the new owner of a baseball team takes a chance on a misfit players like Mike Riley an ex superstar pitcher from this club was sent to the minors two years ago and hasn't been back ever since, Roger Punjaab an Indian American doctor who works for his father decided to join the majors, David Yoder an ex communicated Amish boy from Lancaster decided to leave the community to play Baseball League, Jeff Riley, Riley's father who was a junior college baseball star who became an architect and took his little league baseball team that his firm sponsored to a little league championship. He got laid off from his job for six months and offered to be a manager of the big leagues and Matt Schultz a college baseball and cape league star who ended up as a librarian in the New York Public Library dreams about playing in the Baseball League. He was invited to spring training by accident when they're was another

Schultz that was invited to spring training. These are the players he invites to camp who can turn this team around with a two year losing streak against a greedy corporate raider named Dalton Reynolds who hates the Yankees and wants to tear down the stadium build condos and hotels that will make him a fortune. Ryan is on a mission to save his team from a greedy investor who made a bet if this failing team wins the pennant he invest a lot of money in the team and if he loses he'll tear it down. With this new loser team for winning the pennant is a million to one. But I hope the fans and the city are ready for them.

MATT SCHULTZ is a twenty-eight year old librarian who works in the New York Public Library, who just exiting the subway station and head to the Red Sky Bar tonight to meet his friends. It's one of the top sports bar in New York and home of the The Runaway Boys. Zack is a nerdy guy who used dreamed about playing for the major leagues and the dream is gone. Everybody is watching an old Yankees game on ESPN classics inside the Red Sky Sports Bar and Matt enters the Red Sky and sees his best friend RICK from college sitting in the bar stool and goes over to sit with him. MATT sees his best friend and tells him, "Hey Rick?" RICK tells Matt, "Hey Matt?" MATT tells Rick, "How's work?" RICK tells Matt, "Trust me working as Executive Vice President at Apple in the New York Division is really tough." MATT tells Rick, "I heard you guys are designing a new video system for the company?" RICK tells Matt, "You can forget about you tube or web casting. We built system for people to easier way web casting your show and make some money with it." MATT tells Rick, "Like how?" RICK answers Matt, "You can search for easy video, register for web casting and pay one hundred dollars fee to have your own web casting show on the internet. It will be around the world, once gets in the market." MATT tells Rick, "You told me, if people want to make money by web casting, how you do that?" RICK tells Matt "Simple you can pay a fifty dollar, click money video where people can pay to watch your show each week for 1.99 or 2.99. It depends on the viewers who pays to watch the show". MATT tells Rick, "If they don't make any money in web casting." RICK tells Matt, "They can turn off money video, just web cast for free. Change your web casting, the viewers come back and you click on money video and pay another fifty dollars. You'll make your money on the web." MATT tells Rick, "Sounds pretty cool." RICK tells Matt, "That's the reason, why we call it easy video and easy money video." MATT tells Rick, "How long is going to take to get started?" RICK tells Matt, "It probably won't be out until summer, we still have to look for spokesman to advertise easy video." MATT tells Rick, "Well good luck." The bartender who just finished pouring drink for his customer and puts it under the table. The BARTENDER sees Matt and goes over talk to him. BARTENDER tells Matt, "Hey Matt, can I get you anything?" MATT tells Gary, "I'll take a bud light, Gary!" BARTENDER ask Matt, "Mug or Bottle." MATT tells Gary, "I'll take the bottle." Gary tells Matt, "You got it." Gary sees the fridge, opens it and takes out a bottle of bud light. Gary closes the fridge door, sees the bottle opener and grabs it by his left hand. Gary opens the bottle cap, gives the bottle of bud light to Matt. Matt grabs the bud light from Gary and observes it for a minute. MATT tells Gary, "Thanks Gary." GARY tells Matt, "Hey, no problemo." Matt starts drinking his beer and Gary ask Matt a question. GARY tells Matt, "Hey Matt, you told me yourself you were a college baseball star. You took your team to College World Series team in Fresno State and also Cape League Championship in Harwich Mariners". MATT tells Rick, "Yeah, it was a long time ago." RICK tells Gary, "You were College World Series MVP in 2008 and MVP in Cape League Championship in 2009." GARY tells Rick, "Yeah, in the paper. You told me, you wanted to play for Boston Red sox after Cape Leagues. You were drafted for the league after the scout saw you Cape League Championship after that." MATT tells Gary, "Red Sox, also offered me five million in signing bonus." GARY tells Matt, "No way!" Matt laughs a little for a minute and stops. MATT tells Gary, "Just playing you, Gary." GARY tells Matt, "Funny, Matt. Funny." RICK tells Matt, "So, how much did they offer for a signing bonus Matt?" MATT tells Rick, "Eight hundred thousand dollars, Rick." RICK tells Matt, "I think that was about right. You told me yourself, you got injured when you were doing the infield fly homerun." MATT tells Gary, "That's kind of how I lost my shot for the Red Sox." GARY tells Matt, "We saw the play Matt, how you got injured doing the infield fly homerun that you helped the

Mariners won the championship. So, tell me in your own words what happened." MATT tells Rick, "Well, it's a long story Gary. I played for the Infield Fly homerun, I never thought I could do it. But I took a chance." RICK tells Matt, "We got some time, Matt. Go ahead and tell us." MATT tells Rick during Flashback, "Well, I'm not going to bore you in details. I just get right to the story, before I made the run. It all started top of the ninth and we were playing against the Chatham Anglers and it all started three years ago. Matt flashback at 2009 in Harwich Mariners Baseball Field in Cape League Championship when Matt tells his story to Gary. Matt was a shortstop and the pitcher was about to the throw the ball to Number 21 Hardwick whose on bat. MATT'S VOICE tells Gary, "This was the big game that give me a shot in the major leagues. Back in high school, I was the water boy in baseball team. Our team made it to the district championship, one of our batters got injured with a bad arm. Since, their nobody else to pinch hit. When the Coach saw me, he ask me to fill in. That's how my life changed back then, when I helped my team win District and got me a scholarship to Fresno State and took my team to a College World Series in 2008. I tried out for the Mariners in the Cape League that would guarantee me a shot for the majors. Here I am to the championship. We had two outs, Linwood was on the mound and Hardwick is at bat. Linwood made the pitch and Hardwick hit it hard." Linwood threw the ball and Hardwick swung his bat and hit the ball halfway near between second and third base. Matt who was a shortstop, caught the ball by his and got him out by throwing the ball to first base before Linwood made it. MATT'S VOICE tells Gary, "I caught it. Trust me, that ball that Hardwick hit was really hard, but I caught it and threw it in first base and got him out. That was the last out and it was our turn to bat." Matt watched his teammates trying to win the championship. His first teammate is ready to bat. MATT'S VOICE tells Gary, "This was the bottom ninth of the inning, we were tied 2-2 and all we need was a run to win. If the A's get three outs and they win the championship. There was a major league scout from the Red Sox who was watching the game and is considering recruiting for his team. They offered eight hundred thousand for me, if I win this championship. My career will be set for life." The A's pitcher struck out Matt's first teammate in home plate. MATT'S VOICE tells Gary, "Linwood, struck out Sanderson in home plate. Jesse is up at bat now." Jesse is ready to bat right now, with A's pitcher Linwood on the mound. He throws the ball and strikes him out on the first pitch. MATT'S VOICE tells Gary, "Linwood, had a great arm for the A's. They're probably going to name him MVP is he wins. Trust me, that guy threw it ninety-eight miles per hour. That's usually normal rookie pitchers usually throw." Linwood already got the second strike on Jesse. Linwood throws another pitch and strikes out Jesse at bat. MATT'S VOICE tells Gary, "Linwood threw another pitch and Jesse got struck out. Guess whose up to bat." MARINER'S MANAGER observes the game on the field right now, turns around and see Matt sitting down in the dugout. MARINER'S MANAGER tells Matt, "You're up Schultz." Matt gets up from his seat, sees the bat boy in the dugout and talk to him. MATT ask Billy, "So, Billy what do you recommend?" BILLY grabs the third bat, batters box and gives it to Matt. Matt grabs the bat and observes it for a minute. BILLY tells Matt, "Go for number three, it will give more zing when you hit out of the park." MATT tells Billy, "I'm not going to hit it out of the park." BILLY tells Matt, "You're going inside?" MATT tells Billy, "I'm going inside." BILLY tells Matt, "Good luck, Matt." MATT tells Billy, "Thanks Billy." Matt exit's the dugout and head to home plate. MATT'S VOICE tells Gary, "Here's it is, my opportunity to go to the Major Leagues. They called me the Inside Guy. Because I usually hit inside the park homeruns. For this season, I hit 41 inside the park home runs. I just hit two of them in this game." Matt is in home plate and ready to bat. MATT'S VOICE tells Gary, "That's usually, what I was good at. Hitting inside the park homeruns. I never hit one out of the park before. I don't have the muscle power to hit out of the park. But I do have speed that would give me time run all four bases without being out." Linwood is on the mound and sees Matt on home plate. Linwood looks through his signals by his catcher and got the signal what he's looking for. MATT'S VOICE tells Gary "Linwood, pitched to me five times. The only time, he ever got me out three times, is usually pop flies. I always hit the inside the park home run over his head two times. This time will be number three." Linwood throws the pitch, Matt swings his bat and the umpire calls a strike. The catcher throws the ball back to the pitcher on his first strike. MATT'S VOICE tells Gary, "I got the first strike on purpose, but Linwood threw it really hard. Only because I wasn't ready back then." Linwood threw the second pitch really hard and Matt swings his bat and gets a second strike by the umpire. The catcher throws the ball back to the pitcher again. MATT'S VOICE tells Gary, "Okay, I was blinded by that pitch. But not this time, this was my senior year in college and this is my chance to get in the majors. If I blew this opportunity, I'll never get a shot like this again. But, I decided try something new. That I never did, I usually hit it inside the park, but this time I got a better trick in my sleeve." Linwood throws the pitch, that's really hard and Matt swings it and hit's the ball like a infield fly. The infield fly ball is in fair area, Matt still has a chance to run to base. Matt starts running to first base. MATT'S VOICE tells Gary, "Call me crazy, this was the first time I ever hit a infield fly homerun. I was the second guy who hit a infield fly homerun and that was Babe Ruth." Matt ran all the way to second, third and fourth base. The infield fly ball came down on the field, near the third base and the third baseman grabbed it from the field. Matt was running all the way to the home plate.

The third baseman threw the ball really hard to the catcher in home plate. Matt ran all the way to home plate, but his right knee was hurting really hard. MATT'S VOICE tells Gary, "That infield fly homerun, didn't just win me a championship." Matt slide through home plate, before the catcher tags him out after the ball was thrown to his glove by the third baseman and the umpire makes the call. HOME PLATE UMPIRE tells Matt, "Safe!" Everybody in the stand was cheering, Matt was thrilled that his team won the championship and sees the Boston Red Sox scout is really pleased with him. MATT'S VOICE tells Gary, "Not only, did I win the championship and impressed the Red Sox scout. I waited my whole life to play for the Red Sox and the major leagues. But there was one problem." Matt tries to get up, but his right knee was hurting and starts aching. Matt can't get up from home plate. The Mariner's manager sees Matt hurting and starts yelling for the trainer. MARINER'S MANAGER tells Billy "Billy, get the trainer here now." Mariner's manager and a few of Matt's teammates tried to get me up. MATT'S VOICE tells Gary "I blew my knee out, running all four bases. I done this a hundred times before, I wanted to ask why I hurt my knee doing this again. I can tell you, I call it the Infield Fly Curse. That was my career, my bad knee cost me a shot in the majors when the doctor told me I was out for the next season and I can't be in spring training or play in the minors next season." Back to the present at Red Sky Sports Bar. Matt finishes talking to Gary and Rick about how he lost his shot in the majors in the bar. MATT tells Gary, "Linwood got my spot for the Red Sox and that's how I got here hanging out here with you guys." GARY tells Matt, "So, Matt. I knew you work in the New York Public Library as a librarian, that's how I met you and we used to be die hard Red Sox fans, before we switched to The Runaway Boys." MATT tells Gary, "That was three years ago, when I interned in the library when I was in college. Gary, you were checking out a book about the Yankees, we both used to be Red Sox fans and we decide to switch to Yankees when we both move to New York. You invited me to the sports bar and that's how we became friends and I invited my best friend Rick who was my roommate in college to this bar." RICK tells Matt, "That's how all of us became friends for three years." MATT tells Rick, "Right now, I'm the new acting head librarian since my boss spending his summer vacation in a baseball camp in California. He's one of the counselor there." RICK tells Matt, "I can't believe your boss left you in charge of the Library." MATT tells Rick, "Rick, I'm a valuable employee there. Everybody likes me there, I'm usually guy people usually are friends with." RICK tells Matt, "Too bad, I wish that could help you in your social life." MATT tells Rick, "I wish I have one, I been working in the library and watching home games of the Yankees for the last two years of my life. I have season tickets of the game." GARY tells Rick, "How did you get the season tickets anyway, Matt?"

RICK tells them, "They're mine. The company are die hard Yankees fans and the company always give the tickets to me. Every time, I have to work late. I usually give the tickets to Matt." GARY tells Rick, "That explains why me and Matt go to the games." MATT tells Rick, "Too bad, their always in the nosebleed section." RICK tells them, "Hey, is it my fault my computer firm, can only afford that section if they want to save a few bucks." MATT tells Rick, "Another words, your boss is cheap." RICK tells Matt, "I would've said yeah!" GARY tells Matt, "Trust me, if Matt didn't blew out his knee. Not only we get season tickets from him, he probably get us better seats." RICK tells Matt, "Like dugout seats or luxury suites for your special fans." MATT tells Rick, "If I did play for the Yankees, if I didn't hurt my knee. I would've given you guys the dugout seats." RICK tells Matt, "Thanks Matt, we appreciate that." GARY tells Matt, "So, Matt do you still miss the game?" MATT tells Rick, "Everyday Gary. My knee is fine, it took me a whole year of physical therapy and but I made it through." RICK tells Matt, "How come you didn't go back and try out for the minors for the Red Sox or any other major league." MATT tells Gary, "I don't know Rick, I think I'm a little rusty. It's been two years, I've been out of the field, I don't know if I still have it. Even if I tried out for the red sox or any other team. I probably wouldn't make it. These guys are faster and younger than me who tried out usually get rejected. I probably be humiliated in a heartbeat if I don't make the team. You're looking a twenty-three year old guy, probably be cut in the first try out." GARY tells Matt, "You never know if you don't try." MATT tells Gary, "Trust me, Gary. I tried everyday, I don't think I would be keep up with those guys. I lost my shot, ever since I blew me knee out in the Cape League championship. So, this is my life. I just acting head librarian of the New York Public Library, nothing wrong with it. there is a lot of good people who work their. I'm doing it, I've have nothing to be ashamed. So, this is my life. I'm happy I really am." Gary looks at Matt for a minute and he's not buying it. GARY tells Matt, "Really!" MATT tells Rick, "I told you guys, I happy really am!" RICK tells Matt, "Yeah right." MATT tells Rick, "Really I am." Matt thinks for a minute and whispers to himself. MATT Whispering to himself, "If I only had one shot to play in the Majors, I'll die a happy man." Back in The Runaway Boys Boardroom in the front office of The Runaway Boys. Six members of Yankees Executive staff are sitting down in their chairs in the boardroom table and waiting for the owner to arrive. Yankees General Manager talks to one of the BOARD MEMBERS in the board room. YANKEES GENERAL MANAGER tells George, "So George, when is the new boss going to arrive?" GEORGE tells Terry, "I don't know Terry, the way I look. He's not in a good mood." TERRY tells George, "We were in last place this year. We were again the other year. He's not goanna be happy, about how this club is doing." GEORGE tells Terry, "We were in last place for two years, we lost our best players into free agency when they asked to be traded from this club. This club is been falling apart for two years." TERRY tells George, "There has to be away to turn this club around." GEORGE tells Terry, "How this club is been losing for three years straight. Are best players were arrogant jerks, who treat this club like their own playground." TERRY tells George, "Think about the demands they want?" GEORGE tells Terry, "A five million bonus, their own private jet, a membership to Greenwich country club and a 2012 Porsche Turbo. Talk about outrageous demands." TERRY tells George, "We told those jerks no, they decided to be traded to the Florida Marlins and the owner of that club gave them all their demands that we can't give them." GEORGE tells Terry, "Yeah, I know why. Those guys think are like bullies who shoves our faces in the dirt, because we don't want to give them our lunch money." TERRY tells George, "They're like spoiled brats, if we give in. Besides, we were still in last place when they're here. If we give in any of that stuff, they'll still be in last." GEORGE tells Terry, "Since, those guys are being traded from other teams. Half of the players, don't have the chops to get us out the hole we been in two years. I think we'll have to forfeit the season, since we have no way out of getting out of last place." TERRY tells George, "Hey, I'm sure the new boss will figure something out." GEORGE tells Terry, "The new boss is going to be kicking our faces in the dirt if we don't do something." One of the Yankee board members hears somebody coming in. YANKEES BOARD MEMBER tells them, "Guys, worry about who the boss is going to kill later. Because he's already on his way." The door opens and the new YANKEES OWNER arrives in the board room and talks to the board members about how to turn this team around. The Yankees Owner is a guy who is in late twenties and looks like a computer geek from the software. YANKEES TEAM OWNER tells them "Hello gentlemen, welcome to a new season of the The Runaway Boys." TERRY tells the new boss "Hey kid, who are you?" YANKEES TEAM OWNER tells them, "My name is Ryan Green, I'm the new owner of this club." The board members starts laughing for a minute. TERRY tells Ryan "Yeah right, you're the new owner of this club. If you're the new owner, I'm Clint Eastwood." RYAN tells Terry "Very funny, what's your name buddy?" Everybody stops laughing for a minute. TERRY tells Ryan, "Terry Hunter, the Yankees General Manager of this club. I don't know how you got in here, if you don't leave and shut up. I will call security and have you thrown out of here." RYAN tells Terry, "You wouldn't say that, if I was the new boss. And since I am, Hunter if you don't shut up and I will call security and have you thrown out of this club." TERRY is Laughing and tells Ryan, "Oh yeah, I'm really scared. By the way, if you're the new owner. Where's Ronald Langley, the guy who bought the club and the man we met a few months ago." RYAN tells Terry, "Ronald is my Executive

Vice President of my software firm that I own when I built that place when I was seventeen of a computer that made better DOS and CD-ROM software called Green Tech." GEORGE tells Ryan, "Green Tech, that's the company that is owns the New York Yank…?" George is totally shocked for a minute and so does everyone else. Terry is still laughing for a minute. GEORGE tells Ryan, "Oh god, you're thee Ryan Green who owns this team." RYAN tells George, "That's right, what's your name pal?" GEORGE tells Ryan, "George Jackson, sir. I'm the head of marketing here." RYAN tells George, "Well, George. You just been promoted to the General Manager of this team." Ryan stops laughing and realize that Terry is serious. TERRY tells Ryan, "General Manager, that's my job." RYAN tells Terry, "Exactly, Hunter. George is in and you're out." TERRY tells Ryan, "You really are the new owner, I don't get it. I thought Ronald Langley was the owner of this club." RYAN tells Terry, "I bought this team a few months and I asked Ronald managed this team for me. While I was running my company, since I saw this team falling in last place for two years. I think it's time I step in and I take over. And Terry..?" Terry interrupts Ryan for a minute. TERRY tells Ryan, "Please don't fire me, I'll do anything you need. I have a wife and two kids to support. Please don't fire me." RYAN tells Terry, "Relax Hunter, I'm not goanna fire you." TERRY tells Ryan, "You're not, what a relief." RYAN tells Terry, "You'll be selling hot dogs in opening day this season. After opening day, you'll be back as a marketing executive of this company instead of being back as the general manager. You know why I'm pushing you back as marketing executive." TERRY tells Ryan, "No, why sir." RYAN tells Terry, "Because, George gives me respect here. Unless you don't apologize to me, you still will be marketing executive of this club for the rest of your tenure. If you do apologize to me you can be Co-General Manager of the club. But don't think about apologizing right now, you can apologize to me for the rest of the season." TERRY tells Ryan, "Apologize to you, forget it." RYAN tells Terry, "Okay, enjoy being a marketing executive and by the way. You'll be selling hot dogs for a month this season and then you'll be a marketing executive. How about that." Terry starts to mumble for a minute. RYAN tells Terry "What did you say, I can't hear you." TERRY is Mumbling and Ryan, "Yes sir!" RYAN tells Terry, "Now, let's get on to business." Ryan starts sitting down in his chair on head of the boardroom table. Ryan starts getting down in business. RYAN tells George, "All right, guys. I know we've been in losing streak last year." GEORGE tells Ryan, "Actually Mr. Green, it's been two years we've been in a losing streak." RYAN tells George, "Call me Ryan, George." GEORGE tells Ryan, "Okay Ryan." RYAN tells George, "Tell me, George why we have been in a losing streak in two years?" GEORGE tells Ryan, "Bad management, we have eight players whose are top in their game with their big egos, disrupting this team into last place and our old manager encourage this. Luckily for us, there were other teams wanted take them off our hands." RYAN tells Evan, "You know, George that's amazing. But one problem, those guys are superstars and without them there would be no crowd and we can lose paid attendance." EVAN tells Ryan, "Sir, if we had them. All paid attendance been way down for a long time. That's one of the main reasons, why were in a losing streak right now." RYAN tells Evan, "We've been winning pennants and world series. Ever since this team sold Babe Ruth from Boston in 1920. The The Runaway Boys never would've been here if it wasn't for him. Without Ruth, we never had Mickey Mantle, Joe Dimaggio, Roger Maris, Reggie Jackson, Roger Clemens, Lou Gehrig and Derek Jeter here. Evan ask me again, how we got these to guys to play here and turn this team into best major league team in the world?" EVAN tells Ryan, "Mostly, from scouting and we found their talents when we invited them to spring training." GEORGE tells Ryan, "That was the time, when they're playing for the minors. Gambled with this club to trade them here for this team." RYAN tells Evan, "These big shot players we had, ruined everything baseball stood for. Now baseball is all politics and a lousy steroid scandal. But we overcame this and it's time we bring the Yankees back the way it is." EVAN tells Ryan, "How we do that sir." RYAN tells George, "I'll tell you in a minute, Evan. But I have some news for you guys. Since we lost our top players in free agency. We've been in last place for two years and we've never been out of this slump like ever in two years. But that's goanna change, because I'm running this club now and I watched your old boss drag this team down in the pit. So, I have a proposition for you guys." GEORGE tells Ryan, "So, what's the proposition sir?" Ryan snaps his fingers for a minute, his bodyguard opens the door and enters the boardroom and carrying a list of players who are inviting to spring training on paper on his left hand. Ryan's bodyguard gives the list to Ryan. RYAN'S BODYGUARD tells Ryan, "Here you go, boss!" Ryan grabs the list from his bodyguard and observes it for a minute. Ryan tells Lou, "Thanks Lou!" LOU tells Ryan, "I appreciate that, sir." Lou exit's the boardroom and closes the door. Ryan hands out the list to George and passes around to the board. RYAN tells George, "We have one season to turn this team around, and get this team to a pennant or a world series. I have no choice to sell this team to Reynolds Industries." GEORGE tells Ryan, "Reynolds Industries, isn't that company owned by Dalton Reynolds." RYAN tells George, "That's him, George." GEORGE tells Evan, "He's the biggest corporate raider in New York. This guy is like a wrecking ball. He buys companies like this and demolish this in a heartbeat." EVAN tells George, "Reynolds, wants to buy this team. Why?" GEORGE tells Ryan, "I heard he hates the Yankees, the Mets and baseball for all reasons." RYAN tells George, "He wants to buy this property for condominiums and apartment complex in this area. This is the piece of land he wants, that's going to quadruple his revenue and equity of the place if he bought it." GEORGE tells Evan, "Besides, if he buys the team. He can dismantle this team for good if he buys it. Since, he's not a Yankees fan." EVAN tells Ryan, "So, Mr. Green why are you selling this team to Mr. Wrecking ball? I thought you were a Yankees fan." RYAN tells George, "I am a Yankees fan. When I was a kid, I watched 1999 World Series in Yankees Stadium. With my dad. He and I both love the Yankees. But we've been in a losing streak for two years, this club is ruining my company and this town. That's the reason, why I want to turn things around in this club." GEORGE tells Ryan, "Still don't get why you want to sell this team to Reynolds in the first place. Don't you have any other buyers?" RYAN tells them, "I did, have of them are Yankees fans. But they don't want to take a big chance on buying this team, since we've been in a losing streak for two years. They could lose millions if they buy this team. It's one of the main reasons, why Reynolds is interested in buying this team. There is also something else, I made a deal with Reynolds with this team?" GEORGE tells Ryan, "What deal, Ryan?" RYAN tells Evan, "I made a deal with them, if I turn this team around and get this team to win a American League Championship and go to the world series. He'll invest one hundred million dollars in this team to keep this team a float for a long time and I can stay be the owner of this team and you guys have a lifetime contract renewals. It means, all of you guys will have jobs for a long time." EVAN tells Ryan, "If you lose?" RYAN tells Evan, "I have no choice to sell this team to him. Everybody in this organization will be out of work. All the players and coaches will be sent to the minors, given their release or being traded to another team." EVAN tells Ryan, "You're betting a lot for this team, Mr. Green." RYAN tells George, "Since my company is losing money, when I bought this team. It's time I take a chance. Look, if Colonel Jacob Rupert had to take a big gamble to buy Babe Ruth from Boston. We can take this chance." GEORGE tells Ryan, "Ryan, how is exactly are we getting this team to the pennant." RYAN tells them, "Look at all of the players I know today are egotistical and arrogant jerks. I don't want them in my team. They usually forget who there are and where they come from. So, the only way get to the pennant is looking for underdog players that were going to give a shot to play in the majors." The board starts laughing for a minute. GEORGE tells Ryan, "Yeah, right. This is The Runaway Boys, real life. Not the movie Rocky, Ryan." RYAN tells them, "First of all, stop laughing. Unless you guys want to stand on the unemployment line right now." Everyone stops laughing for a minute. GEORGE tells Ryan, "Sorry boss!" RYAN tells them, "Okay, we forgot about the game and how people use to love of the game. It's what America used to stood for back then. We can get it back. I know how." EVAN tells Ryan, "How is that sir?" RYAN tells George, "I'll show you Evan. The list that George is show

how were going to win the pennant and turn this team around. Is by the inviting these players to spring training and give them a shot to play in the majors." GEORGE tells Ryan, "Half of these guys, I never heard of. The rest of them, I do know are usually has-beens. You want to invite these guys to spring training." RYAN tells them, "Exactly, if we're going to turn this team around. We need the best players and the best are these guys." EVAN tells Ryan, "These players were inviting to spring training are not exactly major league material. You want to invite these guys." RYAN tells them, "That's why I like them. Because these guys are my kind of guys. I want them in spring training, you guys make the call." EVAN tells Ryan, "Yes sir." Ryan gets up from his chair and was about to leave until he talks to board for one minute. RYAN tells them, "You guys, we have one season. To turn this team around and get them to the pennant, if we fail. This stadium and this team will be new condominiums if we lose this wager to Reynolds. You guys better get started." GEORGE tells Ryan, "Yes sir. Ryan heads to the door, opens it and exit's the boardroom and closes the door. Everybody starts reading the list and gets started to invite these players to spring training. Back in Ryan's office in Yankees Stadium. Ryan is sitting down in his chair and Ryan is working in his desk, until he hears a door knock. RYAN tells this person, "Come in." The door opens and it's George. George enters Ryan's office and closes the door and goes over talk to him. RYAN tells George,

"Hey George!" GEORGE tells Ryan, "Hey Ryan!" George sits down in his seat and talks to Ryan. GEORGE tells Ryan, "You know Ryan, one thing I wanted to ask?" RYAN tells George, "Sure, what is it George?" GEORGE tells Ryan, "I understand the players that were inviting to spring training. I know I'm the new General Manager, I wanted to ask whose the new manager of this club?" RYAN tells George "Simple, I'm planning to recruit Jeff Riley as our new manager?" GEORGE tells Ryan, "Never heard of him." RYAN tells George, "I done some research on him, he used to be Junior College World Series Champion in baseball 1964. GEORGE tells Ryan, "At least, I know this guy has some baseball experience. What does this guy know about managing a Baseball League team?" RYAN tells George, "Simple. I read about him after he got drafted here in Yankees after his team won the championship. He blew his knee out while trying to make a triple in the minors and cost him a shot in the majors. He's an architect in a top architecture firm, in Princeton New Jersey. He coaches a little league team that the firm sponsors and took his team to a three little league championship. These players were underdogs and nobodies on earth would pick these kids for this team. But he took a chance on them, made them into champions. He worked three top worse players and help them motivate them to be great and made them champions." GEORGE tells Ryan, "You want to recruit a little league coach to manage a Baseball League team." RYAN tells

George, "Exactly, that's the guy who I want to manage this team. That's who I want, go get him George." GEORGE tells Ryan, "Are you sure about this Ryan." Ryan gives George, Jeff Ryan's number to George and George grabs it and observes it for a minute. RYAN tells George, "That's his number. Make the call." GEORGE tells Ryan, "Okay, if you insist." George gets up from his chair and is about to exit from the door. Until Ryan says something and stops. RYAN tells George, "Good luck George!" George laughs for a minute. GEORGE tells Ryan, "Yes sir!" George stops laughing and heads to the door. George opens the door, exits Ryan's office and closes the door. Back in Lincoln Architecture Designs firm where Jeff Riley works. JEFF is in his late sixties is working in his architecture board on his desk and looks at the design to create a new investment banking company in his office. JEFF tells himself, "I finally finished." Jeff's colleague enters his office, sees Jeff and goes over to see him. JEFF'S COLLAGUE tells Jeff, "Hey Jeff!" JEFF tells Lyndon, "Hey Lyndon!" LYNDON tells Jeff, "You got the design for the new bank yet, Milo is been expecting the designs today?" JEFF tells Lyndon, "Yeah, I'm finished. Here they are?" Jeff grabs the design with both hands and gives it to Lyndon. Lyndon grabs the design from Jeff and observes it for a minute. LYNDON tells Jeff, "Hey, these are amazing. Milo is really pleased with the results, since we landed that Buggy Bank account." JEFF tells Lyndon, "Yeah, it's a billion dollar account. A lot of major architecture firms trying to land that account and we got it." LYNDON tells Lyndon "You did all the work, to get this account. But, I'm sure it will be worth it." JEFF tells Lyndon, "I know, Milo is going to get the partnership when he land this account, for the work that I do for him." LYNDON tells Jeff, "And all the other designs and all the work you do for him. You're the one, who lands those big accounts that gives him promotions and he still treats you like a…?" Jeff interrupts Lyndon for a minute. JEFF tells Lyndon, "Like his workhorse." LYNDON tells Jeff, "I was going to say slave, but workhorse is more like it." JEFF tells Lyndon, "But that's going to change, but when I show him these designs. Since he's the Project Leader and I'm the project manager. Their might be an opening for his job as the project leader in this firm and a huge bump in raise with that. Trust me, he'll give it to me." LYNDON tells Jeff, "I hardly doubt it, Jeff. He's been treating you like a nerd doing his homework, ever since you took this internship from this firm when you were in college and made you his pushover after you graduated." JEFF tells Lyndon, "Look, I know I've been pushed around by him since I first worked here. I've been slaving in this office from him for a long time and he takes all the credit that lands him the big promotions and I end up being his personal assistant instead of the project manager. I never complained, until now." LYNDON tells Jeff, "How come you never report to the C.E.O. that you been doing his work for him." JEFF tells Lyndon, "It's my word against his, since I don't have any proof. I hardly doubt, he'll believe a lowly project manager like me to a top project leader that everybody respects in the firm. Plus, the C.E.O. and Milo are golfing buddies, he wouldn't care if I did work for Milo. The C.E.O., will probably make me do his work too." LYNDON tells Jeff, "My mistake. How do you put up with a guy like Milo?" JEFF tells Lyndon, "I've coached this company little league team from a couple championships and the companies softball team to a championship last year that made this firm look good and made it better. Since, I was the one he picked to coach this team to represent this firm. That's one thing I respect about him. But, I know deep down way deep down, he'll give me the credit for this account and the promotion that he promise me. Trust me, this is my day." LYNDON tells Jeff, "Well, good luck with that Jeff. By the way, why did you take this job anyway, since guys like Milo treat you like his slave?" JEFF tells Lyndon, "You know, I got injured in the minors after I got drafted in the Yankees. Since, I lost my shot. I decided to go back to college and get my degree. I took that internship here in my senior year where I met Milo. He told me, if I stick with him. I'll be in top of the world, when he gets there." LYNDON tells Jeff, "Man, were you wrong. You worked in this firm for a 48 years since, he gets promoted and he leaves you behind. Can you believe that?" JEFF tells Lyndon, "Well, not this time. He promise me this promotion, I'll get it. Besides I wanted to play for the Yankees. But I lost my shot, the only joy I have here. Is coaching little league and companies softball team to both championships. That's the only thing that ever made me happy. If I ever had to coach baseball team anywhere, I would leave this firm and go there for a minute." LYNDON tells Jeff, "We all have dreams Jeff, we can't always get it. We made are choices and be happy where we are. We don't choose to be here, it chose us." JEFF tells Lyndon, "Now, I have to live with it. Be happy with it. Being here may not be my dream job, but getting that promotion from Milo, will change that." LYNDON tells Jeff, "Okay, I'll take this up from him. I'll let you know, when he gives you the results about your promotion and raise." JEFF tells Lyndon, "Wish me luck, Lyndon." LYNDON tells Jeff, "Trust me, Jeff. You'll get it. See ya, man." JEFF tells Lyndon, "Bye Lyndon." Lyndon exit's Jeff's office and heads to the elevator. Jeff tries to breathe for a minute and thinks. JEFF tells Lyndon, "Trust me, this will be my day." Jeff's phone rings for a minute. JEFF tells himself, "I wondered who that is, it wouldn't be Milo. Lyndon was going to tell me in person." Jeff picks up the phone and answers it. JEFF calls on the phone, "Hello!" George is sitting down in his chair in his desk at his office and talking to Jeff on the phone. GEORGE tells Jeff on the phone, "Excuse me, is this Jeff Riley?" JEFF'S VOICE tells George on the phone, "Yes, I'm Jeff Riley, who are you?" GEORGE tells Jeff on the phone, "I'm George Jackson, the new general manager of the The

Runaway Boys. Our club wants to hire you as our new manager." Jeff is on the phone with George for a minute in his office. JEFF tells George on the phone, "Manager of what?" GEORGE'S VOICE tells Jeff, "The The Runaway Boys." JEFF tells George, "The Baseball League team, not a farm team or a minor league team, I'm managing. An actual major league team the The Runaway Boys." GEORGE'S VOICE tells Jeff on the phone, "Yes!" JEFF tells George on the phone, "Is this a prank call or I think you got the wrong Jeff Riley." GEORGE'S VOICE tells Jeff on the phone, "This is the same Jeff Riley, who took his college team Allegany Community College to a Junior College World Series in 1964, got drafted for the Yankees. Lost your shot, when you got injured tried to run a triple in the minors and also has a son name Mike who was our star major league pitcher and got hurt and spent two years in the minor leagues." JEFF tells George, "That's me." George is on the phone with Jeff in his office. GEORGE tells Jeff on the phone, "Were not joking Jeff, we want you to manage this team?" JEFF'S VOICE tells George, "Why would you want to pick me to manage this team?" GEORGE tells Jeff, "We heard about you, taking your company little league team to a championship. Those players were exactly anybody wouldn't pick for that team. But you turn that rag tag team into champions. We want you to do that for this team. Besides were also inviting your son back in the big leagues. It will be up to you, if he stays or goes back to the majors. I wondered if you considered taking this job." Jeff is on the phone with George for a minute in his office. JEFF tells Jeff, "I don't know, Mr. Jackson. I'll think about it." GEORGE'S VOICE tells Jeff, "Call me George, if you changed your mind. Call me at 212-363-5546." Jeff wrote down the number on a post it that's on his desk. JEFF tells George, "I'll think about it George. Bye!" GEORGE Voiceover tells Jeff on the phone, "Bye Jeff!" Jeff hangs up his phone, sees his number for a minute and thinks about the offer. JEFF tells himself, "Manager of the Yankees, sounds like a prank call to me or was it. Trust me, it's a prank call. Nobody on earth would ever give a Baseball League manager job to a little league coach like me and me deciding that my son stays or head back to the minors. Can you believe that?" Jeff sees Lyndon enters the office and going over to Jeff's cubicle for a minute. JEFF tells himself, "Speaking of managing, I think I might get that promotion after all. I'll be moving on up to a bigger office to a bigger floor." Lyndon goes over to Jeff and talks to him. Lyndon is carrying an envelope on his left hand. JEFF tells Lyndon, "Hey Lyndon, I wondered how'd it go with Milo?" LYNDON tells Jeff, "It went okay, he really love your designs that Buggy Bank will impressed with. Now, the firm is working on building for Buggy Bank for the next nine months. Since we landed that account." JEFF tells Lyndon, "All right, this is what I've been waiting for. So, did Milo say anything else?" LYNDON tells Jeff, "Yes, Mr. Milo wants me to give this to you." Lyndon gives the letter from Milo from Jeff, Jeff grabs the info on Milo and observes it for a minute. Jeff opens the letter and reads it. This doesn't look good for Jeff. JEFF tells Lyndon, "I've been laid off for nine months, I landed a billion dollar big account for them and I also did Milo's work for the last seventeen years and he lays me off for this. I can't believe it!" Jeff is really upset right now. JEFF tells Lyndon, "Lyndon, did you know about this?" LYNDON tells Jeff, "Of course not, he just gave me the letter and told me give it to you. I had no idea, what was in it. If I did, I would've been against it and I would've quit if I found about this." JEFF tells Lyndon, "I'm sorry about that, man. Thanks for sticking by me Lyndon, at least you and I will quit together from that slave driver Milo." LYNDON tells Jeff, "Actually, Jeff. I can't quit, I have a wife and two boys to support. I can't afford to quit." JEFF tells Lyndon, "I understand, Lyndon. I can't believe it, I'm being laid off for nine months. What else can go wrong?" LYNDON tells Jeff, "You have to vacate this office in two hours, or Milo is going to put it in the street." JEFF tells Lyndon, "Nine months, I don't know how I'm going to support myself in nine months without pay." LYNDON tells Jeff, "You have a son in the major leagues, he can support you. Besides you guys do get a long." Jeff tells Lyndon, "Right now, he is in the minors. But he is doing okay, I'll be fine. I have a lot of money saved up and Riley does a good job for taking good care of me." Lyndon tells Jeff, "There you go, and you got nothing to worry about."

Jeff tells Lyndon, "Yeah, but I need to do something with my life and I need to make an income for myself. I can't rely on my son forever. Think about my granddaughter she is in college and Riley and I are supporting her. I want to be there to help her. Make a contribution." Lyndon tells Jeff, "I sure you can find a way put her through college? JEFF tells Lyndon, "I'm sure I can, anyway Lyndon, I was going to ask. Is anyone else being laid off besides me?" LYNDON tells Jeff, "No, just you. They're trying to save some money for this company, since this firm got their big account and Milo got his partnership. He doesn't need you in nine months. After the Buggy Bank deal is over, he'll call you back in nine months." JEFF tells himself, "Aah man!" LYNDON tells Jeff, "I have to get going, Mr. Milo needs his coffee right now. Remember you have to vacate your desk in two hours. Bye Jeff." JEFF tells Lyndon, "Not helping Lyndon!" LYNDON tells Jeff, "Okay then!" Lyndon exit's Jeff's Office. JEFF tells Lyndon, "I really hate my life. I really hate it! What am I going to do now?" Jeff puts his head down for a minute, but sees George's number on his desk and makes the call. JEFF tells George, "Whether this is a prank or not, I'll find out if it's true or not. Hello, George I wondered if Yankees Manager is still available." RILEY who is in early forties, is watching a hockey game on TV and drinking a bottle of bud light on the couch in his mansion. Riley puts his beer down on the coffee table and grabs a bag of Doritos and starts scarfing it. Riley's cell phone rings on his nightstand next to the couch. Riley puts his Doritos on the couch, grabs the cell phone and picks it up. RILEY is on the phone with his agent, "Hello?" RILEY'S AGENT'S VOICE tells Riley on the phone, "Riley, it's Luigi your agent?" RILEY tells Luigi, "Hey, Luigi. What's up?" LUIGI'S VOICE tells Riley, "I have some news for you, Riley?" RILEY tells Luigi, "Is it anything to get anything to be back in the majors" LUIGI'S VOICE tells Riley. "I have some bad news, good news and more bad news." RILEY tells Luigi. "What is it?" LUIGI'S VOICE tells Riley on the phone, "I'll tell you when I get here?" RILEY tells Luigi, "When?" LUIGI'S VOICE tells Riley, "Right now, I'm in your front door!" Riley's doorbell rings for a minute. RILEY tells Luigi, "I'll be there in a minute." Riley hangs up his cell phone, heads to the door and opens it. Riley opens the door and his agent Luigi is waiting for him. Luigi is wearing a suit and Armani sunglasses and is calling Riley on his cell phone. Luigi is in his early thirties and handsome. LUIGI tells Riley, "Hello Riley." RILEY tells Luigi, "Hey Luigi, how you doing?" Luigi and Riley do their fist bumps and stops. LUIGI tells Riley, "I'm good." RILEY tells Luigi, "Come on in." LUIGI tells Riley, "Thanks Riley, I appreciate that." RILEY tells Luigi, "Hey, no problemo." Luigi enters the mansion and Riley closes the door. Riley and Luigi head to the living room, Luigi sits down in the couch and Riley ask him something. RILEY tells Luigi, "Is there anything I can get you?" LUIGI tells Riley, "No, I'm good. I'm going to tell you why I'm here?" RILEY tells Luigi, "So, what's the bad news?" LUIGI tells Riley, "Pepsi called, they're going to cancel your distributorship and they're going to take away your endorsement deal." RILEY Angrily tells Luigi, "What!" LUIGI tells Riley, "So is Reebok, American Express and EA sports. They're all canceling your endorsement deals." RILEY tells Luigi, "What do you mean, I'm losing my endorsement deals. How did this happened?" LUIGI tells Riley, "You've been in the minor league for two years, you've been trying to get your game back in the minors that time. You're pitching game hasn't been the same, since the Yanks sent you back to the minors two years. You've been trying really hard to get your pitching arm back, but no avail. It's one of the main reasons, why the franchise haven't called you back up again. The companies you're endorsing are tired of waiting for you to make a comeback or getting back in the majors, so they're considering dropping you from those deals." RILEY tells Luigi, "I can't believe it, all because they're tired of me waiting to get back in the majors. It was the Yankees management fault they dump me back in the minors in the first place. I don't even know why they dump me there in the first place." LUIGI tells Riley, "You had six suspensions fighting with the umpire and your manager. You've been fined, for drinking in practice and punching out the manager and umpire in the same day. You've been losing pitching game since that day? You haven't been the same ever since." RILEY tells Luigi, "My game hasn't been the same since Monica died and my daughter went off to college." LUIGI tells Riley, "Trust me, I believe it. The general manager, thought about trading you. Since, there is no team wanted to take you. He thought about releasing you, but it was too good for you. So, he had another option." RILEY tells Luigi, "Sending me to the minors was the worse option ever." LUIGI tells Riley, "But I have some good news!" Riley sits down in his couch, grabs his beer and starts drinking it. RILEY tells Luigi, "What's the good news?" LUIGI tells Riley, "The only way you can keep your endorsements and your pepsi distributorship if you go back in the majors." RILEY tells Luigi, "How is that going to help me keep my endorsements, the yanks haven't called me up for two years. I hardly doubt they'll call me up right now." LUIGI tells Riley, "There is a way and here's the good news, I got a call from the new Yankees GM. He's inviting you to spring training this week on Wednesday in Tampa. If you make all the ways to the cuts, you're back in the big leagues." RILEY tells Luigi, "Another words, if I don't get red tagged for the rest of the tryouts. I'm back in the majors." LUIGI tells Riley, "Here's the more bad news?" RILEY tells Luigi, "I was afraid of that, what's the more bad news?" LUIGI tells Riley, "If you do get red tagged, you'll be back in the minors and they won't invite you to spring training anymore." RILEY tells Luigi, "I hardly doubt the Yankees would call me up again for the new three years of my career." LUIGI tells Riley, "Without that Pepsi distributorship and those endorsements. You can't make an income or have nothing to live on without it. Trust me, the companies will drop you if you don't get back in the majors." RILEY tells Luigi, "I can't believe it, I used to make twenty mil a year. Now, ever since I got dumped back in the minors. I'm earning less than that." LUIGI tells Riley, "Well, here's the real pressure cooker. The yanks will pay twenty mil a year, if you make it through spring training for the season. But if you get injured, you get nothing for the season." RILEY tells Luigi, "Aah man!" LUIGI tells Riley, "It's the only way, the Yanks will give you the twenty mil if you make it through spring training. That's the deal I made with them. You have three more years left in your contract, if this team doesn't do good this season. You'll lose your twenty mil for your career, if this team doesn't do good this season." RILEY tells Luigi, "Do I even have a choice in the matter?" LUIGI tells Riley, "You want to keep those endorsements, you have to get back in the majors. You want the twenty mil, if you make it and you don't get injured for the season without losing it. You want to have the twenty mil for three season for your career, this team needs to do good. Without that twenty mil or those endorsements, you're going to lose everything you work for. But it's your choice Riley, what do want to do?" RILEY tells Luigi, "If I want to keep my house and everything here. I have no choice, I'll do it. Call the front office, I'll be their spring training." LUIGI tells Riley, "I knew you can do it." RILEY tells Luigi, "This is so much pressure, but I just hope my pitching game is back after that. Wish me luck." LUIGI tells Riley, "Trust me, Riley. You'll be fine." RILEY tells Luigi, "I hope so." Luigi starts dialing on his cell phone and makes the call to the Yankees. LUIGI tells Riley, "Hello George, good news!" RILEY tells Luigi, "Just hope the Yanks are ready for me. Or I'm ready for them." Riley drinks his bud light beer. Matt is sitting down in his chair in the front desk on the first floor and reading People Weekly magazine. A lady enters the front desk and goes over talk to Matt. LADY IN THE FRONT DESK ask Matt, "Excuse me!" Matt puts his magazine down for a minute on his desk and talks to the lady in the front desk. MATT tells Lady in the front desk, "Hi, can I help you?" LADY IN THE FRONT DESK tells Matt, "I wonder if you guys have a biography of the The Runaway Boys" MATT tells the lady in the front desk, "Biographies are on the second floor and make a right. Go to shelf 135.6 and that's where you can find it." LADY IN THE FRONT DESK tells Matt, "Thank you, I appreciate that." MATT tells Lady in the front desk, "Hey, no problemo." Lady in the front desk leaves and heads to the second floor. Rick and Gary enters the front desk and goes over talk to Matt. Gary is carrying a big envelope on his left hand. RICK tells Matt, "Hey Matt!" MATT tells them, "Hey guys, how are you doing?" RICK tells Matt, "Were good, man." GARY tells them, "I have some good news for you guys?" MATT Sarcastically tells Gary, "Kristen Stewart finally return your calls Gary?"

GARY tells Matt, "Funny, Matt. Funny." MATT tells Gary, "So, what's the good news?" GARY tells Matt, "I got the spring training tickets for the The Runaway Boys for all three of us to watch the games in a couple days." Matt and Rick are shocked and wowed. MATT tells Gary, "The Runaway Boys, thee The Runaway Boys. The Baseball League team that Babe Ruth, Lou Gehrig, Roger Maris and Mickey Mantle played at." GARY tells Rick, "Yep!" RICK tells Gary, "Tell me, you're not playing us?" GARY tells Matt, "Trust me, I'm not." MATT tells Gary, "Tell me, if you're not playing us, this is the same The Runaway Boys spring training area that takes place in George M. Steinbrenner Field in Tampa Florida." Gary puts down the envelope, opens it and sees the tickets of the Yankees Spring Training game in Florida to Matt and Gary. GARY tells Matt, "Read it and weep!" MATT tells Gary, "No way, you're not playing us. These are real, I can't believe it. Tell me Gary where did you get these tickets." GARY tells Rick, "I may not have season tickets like anybody else. But, I ordered them few weeks before spring training starts and got us hotel reservations near George M. Steinbrenner Field before opening day." RICK tells Gary, "It's so amazing, that you have these tickets. I've been trying to get spring training for the last few months, they must have cost a fortune. To get them." GARY tells Rick, "There is one thing, I should tell you guys." RICK tells Gary, "What's that?" GARY tells them, "I only got the tickets for a few games. Were only going to stay in Florida for two weeks." MATT tells them, "That's cool, at least we get to see a couple games. Who knows one of those lucky players might have a chance to play for the majors this time soon." RICK tells Gary, "Just hope they don't get red tagged?" GARY tells Matt, "Red Tagged?" MATT tells Gary, "There are two ways to get in the majors. If you try out for the minors and get in. You play for the minors, you can called up by the majors when major scouts watch you in the game." GARY tells Matt, "What's the second way?" MATT tells Gary, "If any player, gets invited to spring training. We get to show the majors what were made of, if we don't get red tagged during all cuts were in. If you do get red tagged, you're dumped back in the minors. You have to wait until next year to get invited back or wait until the major league calls you up." GARY tells them, "Now, I remember. I heard about that. You know Matt, if you weren't injured you would've been called up in a couple days or make it through the cuts during spring training." RICK tells Matt, "Me too." MATT tells them, "I appreciate that guys. But I lost my shot, I'm okay with it. It's been a while since, I've been out of the field." RICK tells Matt, "You're knee is been healing fine since then." MATT tells them, "Right after a few years, right after I won the cape league championship. Running the inside the park homerun that cost me a shot in the majors when I blew my knee out. Even after my knee was healed, for a couple months since physical therapy. It was too late to go back to college baseball for the scouts to see me. I hardly doubt the coach wanted me back on the field, after what happened to my knee. So I was benched and lost my shot in the drafts." GARY tells Matt, "Even after you graduated from college, how come you didn't just try out for the minors three years ago?" MATT tells Gary, "It was too late, after I finished my internship in the library and got a full time job. I guess I never had any time to try out and plus I don't have the playing edge I used to have back then. I kind of lost it after I got hurt." GARY tells Matt, "You'll never know Matt. If you had another shot to play in the majors, I think you're playing edge would come back." MATT tells Gary, "Gary, I've been out of the field for three years. Even if I tried out again, I don't think I can get it back in one day. Half of the guys I try out with are younger and faster than me. I'll probably laughed at if I ever tried out." RICK tells Matt, "You never know, if you don't get a shot." MATT tells Rick, "Well, I think about it. Even if I try out again next year. I'll see if I can get in or not." RICK tells them, "That's the spirit Matt." GARY tells Matt, "I knew I could count on you." MATT tells them, "Thanks guys, I appreciate that." RICK AND GARY tells them, "Hey, no problemo." Matt sees the pretty girl walks into the library, she wears jeans and a t-shirt and looks practically young. The pretty girl is moving a book cart on the first floor. RICK tells Matt, "Hey Matt are you okay?" MATT tells them, "I'm good, I just lost my head for a minute." Gary sees the PRETTY GIRL for a minute.

GARY tells Matt, "I guess I can see why you lost your head. You really like that girl?" MATT tells Gary, "No, I don't." Gary looks at Matt for a minute. MATT tells Gary, "All right, I like her. A lot." GARY tells Matt, "You know anything about her?" MATT tells Rick, "I don't know, I never met her. I think she's new?" RICK tells Matt, "Well, I know her." MATT tells Rick, "Really who is she Rick?" RICK tells Matt, "I know a couple things, her name is Ashley she's a student in NYU an English major. She's a die-hard Yankees fan and I think her father used to play for the Yanks and I think he was dumped back in the minors. That's all I know about her." MATT tells Rick, "Her dad used to play for the Yankees?" RICK tells Matt, "Yeah!" GARY tells them, "I can't believe Ashley's father used to play for the Yankees. What position he plays, pitchers center fielder or third baseman." RICK tells them, "Well, I don't know Gary. That's all I heard about her." MATT tells Rick, "Rick, how do you know about her anyway?" RICK tells Matt, "Around!" Matt looks at Rick for a minute. RICK tells Matt, "Your boss invested a couple of shares in my company couple days ago. He told me a couple things about her when he hired her after he invited me to his office when I delivered his stock certificates in person for investing in my company." MATT tells Rick, "That explains a lot. Man, it would've been so cool if any guy would love to date her. Whoever she dates will be one lucky guy." GARY tells Matt, "So, Matt why don't you ask her out?" MATT tells them,

"First of all, Ashley looks like a supermodel and I'm a washed up college baseball player who works as a nerdy librarian. There is no way on earth a girl like that would ever date me. Trust me, a girl like Ashley wants perfection." GARY tells Matt, "Let me guess, good looking, successful and the perfect body." MATT tells Rick, "I'm not exactly any of that. Trust me, a girl like that deserves better. Were kind of the guys, fantasizes dating girls like Ashley. Since, I'm the nice nerdy guy. Brooding bad boy types are usually the girls that Ashley dates." RICK tells Matt, "That really sucks." MATT tells them, "I may never get a girl like Ashley to date me, but at least I can fulfill one goal. Me trying out for the major league team. When I try out next year.

Even if I don't get it, but at least I had a shot. At least I can say about Ashley ex-boyfriends. Who are rich pricks that her father would've approved of?" GARY tells Matt, "That's the spirit, Matt." MATT tells Gary, "So, Gary when do we leave?" GARY tells them, "The game doesn't start until two days, we can leave tomorrow morning at ten to the airport. Since, I'm the manager of the bar. I can give myself two week paid vacation." RICK tells them, "Since, I'm the vice president of the company. I did work for a couple years not asking for a day off. I think my boss owes me a couple weeks paid vacation." MATT tells them, "I'm the deputy head librarian. My boss will be out of town for a summer cruise, so I'm in charge for the summer. I guess I give myself a couple weeks off from work since I'm the boss."

GARY tells them, "So, what do you say guys. You guys want to watch a few springing training games in Tampa in two days. MATT tells Gary, "Gary, I got one thing say to you. I'm in." RICK tells Gary, "You had me when do we leave for the airport." GARY tells them, "Let's do it." Matt, Gary and Rick put their fist together and shake. All three of them let go. The airplane lands on the runway at TAMPA INTERNATIONAL AIRPORT. Outside the main entrance in Hilton Garden Inn. Matt is driving his 2011 Ford Taurus rental car where Gary and Rick are in the passenger seats. Matt parks on outside of the main entrance and stops. Matt, Gary and Rick exit's the car and trunk opens. Gary and Rick takes out their luggage out of the trunk for a minute. GARY tells Rick, "First we'll check in, order room service and watch a couple of action flicks. Before we head to the game tomorrow." RICK tells Matt, "It will be so cool, to watch potential players that's going to play in the majors in a few months." MATT tells Gary, "Too bad our tickets only get us a few games. But it'll be worth to watch some games tomorrow." GARY tells Rick, "You think we should head to Daytona tonight, I heard they're a spring break party in the Plaza Resort And Spa. That's where a lot of college kids go to for spring break." RICK tells Gary, "Gary, aren't we little bit old go to spring break party in Daytona. None of us are in college anymore. Even if we were, were young as we used to be as we party." GARY tells Rick, "I heard they were a lot of girls from top sororities from USC, Florida State, University of Miami and Michigan going to the party tonight." RICK tells Gary, "I say, let's go their tonight. You know what I always love about spring break parties. A lot of hot, young girls who are so drunk. They would sleep with anybody." GARY tells Matt, "Hey Matt, what was spring break like for you?" MATT tells Gary, "I never went to spring break. I played baseball for the entire season, why all the other teammates went to frat parties and spring break. I just practiced my game really hard and studied in college." GARY tells Matt, "You sound like some kind of monk." MATT tells Gary, "I wasn't a monk, I was on a baseball scholarship and I have to pass all my classes to play. If I want to stay in school. My dad told me, baseball doesn't pay the bills or put food on the table. So, I had to prove him wrong, when I got that baseball scholarship to Fresno State." GARY tells Matt, "How come your dad hates baseball and how did he let you play in high school?" MATT tells Gary, "Baseball is not a sport that will amount to anything. Football was his sport, he wanted me to play that has a future. Since I didn't have the height or size to play. I usually like playing baseball more than being tackled by three hundred pound guy. I choose baseball, because I love the game. Trust me, we didn't get along and I had to lie to my dad that I was a water boy for a college football team for practice games that will look good on a scholarship." GARY tells Matt, "And he bought it?" MATT tells Rick, "Of course, my coach was friends with Boston university football coach their and he helped me fool my dad since he played baseball in high school there."

RICK tells Matt, "What about the game winning inside the park homerun that won your school a district championship and getting that baseball scholarship to Fresno State. You think he would've found out about it?" MATT tells Rick, "He didn't found out, I told him myself. He was angry and we stopped talking after that. I was about to graduate next month and turn eighteen next week. I didn't even care what he thought, so after our argument. I left home and stayed with my baseball coach who took me in after my fight with my dad. After I graduated, I left for Fresno State and the rest is history." RICK tells Matt, "Man that must've been tough." MATT tells Gary, "That's the reason, why I had to study hard to keep my scholarship and do well in baseball. So, I can play in the major leagues. Show my dad, baseball can amount to something." GARY tells Matt, "How long, has it been since he died?" MATT tells Gary, "It's been a year. I haven't spoken to him, when I went off to college and not look back. But, I don't have any regrets playing in my high school baseball team and going to college and play for their baseball team. I made it to the funeral. Along time, I wish my dad would come see my games and tell me I'm sorry what he said and he was proud of me. That's all I ever wanted from him even if I didn't play for the majors or not." GARY tells Matt, "He may never had a chance to tell you before he died, but I think he always been proud of you." MATT tells Gary, "Thanks Gary, I appreciate that." GARY tells Matt, "Hey, no problemo." MATT tells Gary, "I'll be back in a hour and I want take a look at the stadium before I check in. I always wanted to see wanted to see what spring training looks likes up close when I watch the players practicing." GARY tells Matt, "Okay, no problemo. I call the hotel and leave a key for you at the front desk when you get back. Me and Rick will be heading to Daytona in a few minutes after we check in for the beach party." MATT tells Gary, "Sure thing." GARY tells Matt, "If you change your mind go to the spring break party at the hotel, we'll leave you a train ticket at the front desk." MATT tells Gary, "All right, bye guys." GARY tells Rick, "Bye Matt!" RICK tells Gary, "See ya!" Matt sees his luggage in the trunk, closes it and shakes Rick and Gary's hand and let's goes. Matt opens the door and closes it when he gets inside his rental car. Matt starts the car and exit's the hotel. RICK tells Gary, "Come on, Gar. Let's check in." Rick and Gary carrying their luggage and heads to the door. GARY tells Rick, "What do you think drunken college girls are like in a party?" RICK tells Gary, "Their Desperate and needy and they'll sleep with anybody." GARY tells Rick, "That's why I love Spring Break!" RICK tells Gary, "Me Too!" A lot of fans are watching the players practicing on the field behind on the gate at the George M. Steinbrenner Field. Jeff and George are outside the field and waiting for some of the players to enter for spring training. JEFF ask George, "So, who are the players that was invited to camp?" An young Asian INDIAN BOY parks his 2011 BMW 535i xDrive in the parking lot and exit's his car. Indian kid closes his door, gets his suitcase in the passenger seat when he opens the door and closes it. This young Indian kid enters the camp, wearing jeans and a t-shirt and Armani sunglasses. JEFF tells George, "Whose he? I didn't know you guys have high price talent on this kid?" GEORGE tells Jeff, "He's high price, but not talented. The kid lives off his wealthy father who is a doctor." JEFF tells George, "How did he get invited here?" GEOROGE tells Jeff, "Roger Punjab, his family is from India and he was born and raised in Cherry Hill, New Jersey. His real name is Rajesh, his father was a successful doctor and he wanted his son to be a doctor too. He used to be captain of his baseball team in high school. Took his team to a city championship, that got'em a scholarship to Yale. His father wanted him to be a doctor like him when he goes there and he decided to respect his wishes. But he doesn't want his son to play baseball, that will interfere in his studies and baseball is a waste of time with no future. He'll pay his tuition and if he gives up his athletic scholarship to Yale. He did and went to Yale and Yale Med School for eight years and he finished his residency for four years. His father wanted him to join his practice, he doesn't want to be a doctor anymore, he lied to his father that he's going to Africa for Doctors without Borders for a year. His father understood, he played for the minors for a month, the team decided to invite him to a camp. When a couple of scouts saw him play?" JEFF tells George, "Is he any good?" GEORGE tells Jeff, "The kid hadn't played ball in years. He stunk in the minors, the guy can catch a fly ball, but he is an excellent power hitter, but usually gets struck out a lot by fastballs. But that's not enough to be called up here, but it was Ryan's idea to invite him here. To see if we can work on his fastballs and see what's he got." JEFF tells George, "I guess it's up to me to see if he stays or leaves in this team." GEORGE tells Jeff, "You betcha." A young AMISH KID parks his 2001 Pontiac firebird in the parking lot. This nerdy guy is wearing a suit and glasses, takes out his suitcase out of his car, closes the door and enters the camp. JEFF tells George, "Who's that guy?" GEORGE tells Jeff, "That has to be David Yoder." JEFF tells George, "Yoder, is that mean he's…?" George interrupts Jeff for a minute. GEORGE interrupts Jeff and tells him, "Amish. That's right, he was an excellent centerfielder in baseball. He used to play with the amish kids back then and he was really good. The kid is from Lancaster and he decided to tell his parents, he was leaving the community and to try out for the majors. He played for the Pittsburgh Pirates farm team, he hasn't been called up for a few weeks. The kid really stunk into catching fly balls. Since the Pirates won't call'em up, Ryan took the chance to invite him here to camp." JEFF tells George, "I guess that's one major defect, I can fix." Riley's parks his 2011 Ferrari 599 SA Aperta in the parking lot. Riley exits his car, takes out his suitcase out of his car and closes the door. Riley heads to the camp. Riley is wearing jeans, t-shirt, black jacket and wearing ray ban sunglasses. JEFF tells George, "Hey, isn't that Mike Riley?" GEORGE tells Jeff, "Yeah, that's him. How did you know him?" JEFF tells George, "He's my son." GEORGE tells Jeff, "You're Mike Riley's father. I can't believe it? JEFF tells George, "Even I didn't believe it. He was in the minors for two months. The guy struck out twelve players when he was there. Yankees scout spoke to me when I watched him play. He was impressed and called the GM to call him up, when he strike out three extra players in the final inning. The rest is history. I been proud of him ever since." GEORGE tells Jeff, "Sounds amazing." JEFF tells George, "He was a good son and really good to me." GEORGE tells Jeff, "Riley was an excellent pitcher back then, he blew his arm out in the all star break, they had no choice send him back to the minors. He hasn't been called up in two years." JEFF tells George, "I also heard the other reason, why they send him back to the minors. It had something to do six suspensions fighting with the umpire and his manager. He was also been fined, for drinking in practice and punching out his manager and umpire in the same day." GEORGE tells Jeff, "I hardly doubt it, it was just a rumor." JEFF tells George, "So, how did he do in the minors?" GEORGE tells Jeff, "He gave up a couple of runs when the batter hit a home run off his head. That's what it was like back in two years." JEFF tells George,

"That's explains, why he hasn't been called up back then. We haven't seen each other much, when I was busy as an architect and him sent back to the minors I wish I could helped him back then. But I was so busy with my job and he was busy trying to get back to the majors himself. We don't have time to spend together. Until now." GEORGE tells Jeff, "Ryan took a chance, to invite him here. If he makes through the cuts, he's has one year to make a comeback and keep his endorsements and distribution deal with Pepsi. If he does good and he gets twenty million deal for three years. If he gets injured, he gets nothing." JEFF tells George, "What happens if he gets red tagged?" GEORGE tells Jeff, "He'll lose his endorsement and distribution deals. Without it and his twenty mil contract, he may lose his house and can't pay for his daughter's college tuition, if he gets dumped back in the minors and he can't be invited back to camp anymore." JEFF tells George, "I hardly doubt the club will ever call him up again after he gets cut." GEORGE tells Jeff, "You betcha, that's why…?" Jeff interrupts George for a minute. JEFF tells George, "I know, I know. It will be up to me, if he stays or leaves at this camp." GEORGE tells Jeff, "You got that right?" JEFF tells George, "So George, who's the last guy being invited here?" GEORGE tells Jeff, "I don't know his name, but I think his name is Schultz. But I don't think I know what his first name is." JEFF tells George, "So, anything about this Schultz guy?" GEORGE tells Jeff, "Yeah, he played for

Clearwater Threshers, the Philadelphia Phillies farm team he played for six years. He was a shortstop for that team, not really that good and was a lousy hitter. He hasn't got a hit for the last six years. It's one of the main reasons, he wasn't called up." JEFF tells George, "Maybe we can help this kid out." Matt parks his 2011 Ford Taurus rental car in the parking lot, exit's the car and closes it. Matt sees the stadium and watches every major player practicing on that field. Matt sees George and Jeff near the main entrance where all players who were invited to camp and goes over to meet them. Jeff and George sees him coming this way. GEORGE tells Jeff, "Who is that guy?" JEFF tells George, "I think it might be that Schultz kid?" GEORGE tells Jeff, "I hardly doubt that kid is major league material. Have you seen him? "JEFF tells George, "Me neither, but I think he might be a great asset for this team." Matt goes over to Jeff and George and talk to them. MATT tells Jeff, "Hi, how are you doing? Which one of you guys is the manager of this team?" JEFF tells Matt, "I am." Jeff shakes Matt's hand for a minute. JEFF tells Matt, "I'm Jeff Riley." MATT tells Jeff, "It's a pleasure to meet you, Mr. Riley. I'm a die hard Yankees fan. I used to be a Red Sox fan, growing up in Boston. But I switched teams, when I moved out to New York two years ago." JEFF tells Matt, "I'm happy to hear that, kid." Matt let's goes of his hand for a minute. MATT tells Jeff, "I know this team was in a losing streak for two years and the old manager, drag this team under the mud. But I'm sure, you can turn this team around and get them back to the World Series." JEFF tells Matt, "I'm sure, I could. What's your name, kid?" MATT tells Jeff, "My name is Matt Schultz, sir." JEFF tells Matt, "Well Schultz, we've been waiting for you. Come on in and we've been expecting you." MATT tells Jeff, "I am, wow sounds cool. At least I know you guys know how to treat a fan." JEFF tells Matt, "Before you go in, do you have your luggage? If you don't, we can get you some clothes inside." MATT tells Jeff, "I have it in my car, Mr. Riley." JEFF tells Matt, "Okay, go get it. Matt. Please call me, Jeff." MATT tells Jeff, "Okay, Jeff. Don't go anywhere, I want to show you my inside the park home run." JEFF tells Matt, "I'm sure, I like to see that." Matt goes over to his car and grabs his luggage for a minute. MATT tells himself, "Why would they want me get my luggage, I'm just going to watch them practice. Before I head back to the hotel." Jeff and George looks at Matt for a minute. GEORGE tells Jeff, "I think I found Schultz's first name and Matt's name is not on the list." JEFF tells George, "What was his name that was on the list, George?"

GEORGE tells Jeff, "Axel!" JEFF tells George, "Must be his middle name, he want to put on his list. But put down Matt anyway on the list." GEORGE tells Jeff, "Okay!" George crosses off Axel off the list and put down Matt. Axel Schultz who is driving his 1998 Pontiac Trans Am, who is the real player who was invited to camp and heads to spring training in the Florida Highway. Axel sees a banana, the tires slips and sideswipes and crashes the car way beyond the shoulders and Axel and his car dies. Everybody starts unpacking when they put their clothes on their shelves next to their bunk beds in Yankees Player's Barracks. Riley is almost finishes packing and sees David whose bunk bed is right next to him. Riley goes over to David and talk to him. RILEY tells David, "Hi, my name is Mike Riley. I'm one of the players, whose been invited here and you are?" David shakes Riley's hand for a minute. DAVID tells Riley, "David, David Yoder." RILEY tells David, "How you doing, David?" DAVID tells Mike, "I'm good, Mike!" David let's goes of Riley's hand for a minute. RILEY tells David, "Call me, Riley. If you call me Mike, I won't answer." DAVID tells Riley, "Okay, Riley." RILEY tells David, "Yoder, isn't that Amish?" DAVID tells Riley, "Yes, it is!" RILEY tells David, "Wow, you don't look Amish and you don't have a German or Swiss accent." DAVID tells Riley, "Just my parents who had the accent." RILEY tells David, "So, what are you doing out here? Isn't your community usually against you playing professional sports?" DAVID tells Riley, "It is, I grew up in Lancaster. You know what Rumspringa is?" RILEY tells David, "I heard about that, isn't that where Amish teenagers go out in the English world? Experience things, their religion doesn't allow, you guys have a choice. After it's over, go back home or stay in the English world. I guess, you stayed here?" DAVID tells Riley, "Not quite, I went to Rumspringa in Pittsburgh where I stayed with a couple of relatives who left the order. My uncle took me to this sports bar, where he is a Pirates fan. I fell in love with a game. Man, I loved baseball and me and my uncle went to Pirates games a lot. I always dreamt about playing for the majors. When Rumspringa is over, I chose to go back home, because I don't want to disappoint my father into marrying Katie, the girl I was supposed to marry and my father bought our house next to theirs. I didn't want this to be my life, I see how happy those guys felt, when they played baseball. I used to play it when I was a kid, I used to love hitting the ball out of the park. But when I'm a teenager, I'm not allowed to play it anymore. Because my religion forbids it, I don't want to settle. So, I snuck into high school baseball field where it was empty. Played the game, I was really good, then I met high school coach who saw me play. We kind of bonded, so I spent most of my time learning the game from my coach who taught me the game. I'm not supposed to go there. You know what would happened if the order found out…?" Riley interrupts David for a minute. RILEY tells David, "You would've been shunned and you probably leave the community." DAVID tells Riley, "Exactly, but I want go to high school and get my diploma and play in the majors. So, the coach pulls some strings with the school let me take me my GED and get me a tryout for the pirates. I knew I couldn't tell my parents, so I told'em I had to pick up some food for Katie's family. Anyway, I took the test I passed and I made it to minors. So, I told my father, I'm going to the minors and play for

Baseball League. I'm not going to marry Katie. He was disappointed and the entire community shunned me and that was that. I left for Triple A and the rest is history." RILEY tells David, "If you were playing for minor league baseball for the pirates, what brought you here?" DAVID tells Riley, "I couldn't cut it in the minors, I couldn't catch any fly balls. It's one of the main reasons, why I didn't get called up. Anyway, George the general manager of the Yankees, invited me to spring training and the rest is history. I really want to make this team." RILEY tells Riley, "Good luck, David. The only way, you make this team. If you don't get red tagged." DAVID tells Riley, "I heard about that, if I get a red tag in my locker, near all the cuts. I get sent back to the minors." RILEY tells David, "Exactly, it's going to take you a while to get called up back again." DAVID tells Riley, "You got that right." RILEY tells David, "Welcome to the team, kid." Matt enters the barracks, sees his bunk assignment and Riley. Matt goes over to Riley and talk to Matt and David. MATT tells Riley, "How are you guys doing, I'm Matt Schultz." Matt shakes Riley's hand for a minute. RILEY tells Matt, "Hi, Matt. I'm Mike Riley." MATT tells Riley, "Mike Riley, I heard about you. World Series champ 96, 98, 99 and 2000. Eight time all-star and nominated for cy young eight times. RILEY tells Matt, "Actually it was nine times." Riley let's goes of Matt's hand. MATT tells Riley, "I was a great fan of yours when I was a kid. Hang on a second." Matt sees his suitcase, opens it and takes out his baseball and his pen from his suitcase. Matt shows Riley his baseball. MATT tells Riley, "I wondered if you want to autograph this, Mr. Riley." RILEY tells Matt, "Look, uh Matt. I'm not an autograph mood right now, right now I have to concentrate on spring training." MATT tells Riley, "Please, you're my idol in baseball." RILEY tells Matt, "Okay, anything for a fan." Riley grabs Matt's baseball and pen. Riley autographs Matt's baseball and is done. Riley gives Matt's baseball to him. Matt grabs the ball from Riley and observes it for a minute. MATT tells Riley, "I can't believe it's you, there were rumors that you died. That nobody ever heard from you again." RILEY tells Matt, "Who told you that I died?" MATT tells Riley, "It was in the newspapers, there were rumors that you were dead in 2013. When you didn't showed up on the mound in Yankees stadium." RILEY tells Matt, "God, I hate the press. I didn't die, what's your name kid." MATT tells Riley, "Matt, Mr. Riley!" RILEY tells Matt, "Please call me, Riley and I didn't die, Matt. I was sent to the minors when my pitching wasn't the same as it used to be. You have to love the press, I bet it was my publicist who told everyone I died. I had to fire him for that." MATT tells Riley, "That explains a lot, your pitching hasn't been the same in 2010. When the manager dumped you out of starting rotation." RILEY tells Matt, "It doesn't matter anyway, if I don't make the cuts in Spring Training. I'm sent back to the minors again." MATT tells Riley, "If you get sent back, I hardly doubt the Majors call you up again." RILEY tells Matt, "Not helping Kid. What team you played for?" MATT tells Riley, "Fresno State and Harwich Mariners." RILEY tells Matt, "How'd far you went when you played for these teams?" MATT tells Riley, "College World Series and Cape League Championships. I blew my knee out in the championship game in the Cape Leagues that cost me a shot in the majors." RILEY tells Matt, "How on earth did you get invited to spring training here?" MATT tells Riley, "Just plain lucky and since the new manager invited me here to watch you guys play in person. He probably wanted to work out with you guys in the field." RILEY tells Matt, "What about your knee, you think you can make it in spring training." MATT tells Riley, "My knee is 100 percent, I can still play." RILEY tells Matt, "We'll see what you got kid. Matt, good luck on the team. I'll be there to help you out and I get the bottom bunk and you get the top bunk." MATT tells Riley, "Thanks Riley, I appreciate that." RILEY tells Matt, "We better get some sleep, practice is goanna start tomorrow morning. Good night, Matt." MATT tells Riley, "Good night, Riley." Riley is about turn in for a minute and Matt looks at Riley for a minute. MATT tells Riley, "Man, it's so great to meet one of my favorite players. Why did he ask me questions about my knee and why is he acting like I'm trying out for this team. It sounds like I'm trying out for the majors. I think he was exaggerating, it must be misunderstanding." All the players who are a sleep and Matt is on the top bunk in his pajamas. Matt is reading a Harry Potter book. MATT tells Riley, "I hope my friends are okay. Because I left my cell phone in my car. I think they might be worried about me. I hardly doubt it, I call them in the morning. I wanted to ask, how a guy like Harry Potter can change things in Hogwarts. I have no idea." Matt is wearing his Yankees Uniforms and talking to Roger right next to him, both of them are waiting for 100 yard sprint to see how fast they are in the practice field in George M. Steinbrenner field. MATT tells Roger, "It's so cool to work out with these guys. My name is Matt Schultz and you are?" Roger shakes Matt's hand for a minute. ROGER tells Matt, "Roger! Roger Punjab." MATT tells Roger, "Roger, isn't that short for…?" Roger interrupts Matt for a minute. ROGER tells Matt, "It's Rajesh." MATT tells Roger, "I never knew any Indian Americans who plays Baseball League before." ROGER tells Matt, "Me neither. I'm like an Indian Jackie Robinson. Trust me, my father would never approve of me playing Baseball League." MATT tells Roger, "My dad, either. He told me it was a waste of time. He wanted me to play football. He was a college football star in Stanford and runner up for the Heisman trophy. He wanted me to do that too. Trust me, it wasn't my game. I lied to my father and told him I was the water boy for Boston university football team. Since I played for the high school baseball team, my coach got me the job as a water boy and helped me fool my dad., When my team went to the district championship. Since they don't have any other players on the final inning to bat, the coach put me in and I hit an inside the park home run that won me a championship. That got me a scholarship to Fresno State, I told my dad and he was disappointed in me. We stopped talking after that, I stayed with my baseball coach after graduation. The rest is history." ROGER tells Matt, "Welcome to my world, he let me played high school baseball. It would've looked good on a college application. I was all-city, high SAT scores and honor roll. Since, I took my team to a city championship that got me a baseball scholarship to Yale. But my Dad, didn't want baseball interfere in my studies. He pulled some strings with the dean of admissions that got me enrolled as a regular student and he pay my tuition. That way, I can be a doctor like him. So, I went to Yale and Yale Med School just to make him happy, he was never unaware I was miserable. So, I went to Med school and took up residency in Greenwich. Too make him happy." MATT tells Roger, "Between, med school and residency. How did you end up here?" ROGER tells Matt, "After residency, my father wanted me to join his practice. Being a doctor was his life, not mine. I really wanted to play for the major leagues. So, I told my dad I was offered to work in Africa for Doctors without Borders for a year. I told him, I took it. Anyway, I tried out for the minors and I got in and here I am." MATT tells Roger, "I guess we both have daddy issues. Trust me, even as a fan working out with this team would roll over his grave. Since I probably was the millionth fan, when the manager invited me here to camp and spend a day in spring training." ROGER tells Matt, "Wait a minute, are you saying that you're a Yankees fan. You got in here because the new manager invited you here as a millionth fan." MATT tells Roger, "Yeah, I didn't even showed him my ticket. I guess he was really busy with other players that he had to work with in spring training. Even if I tried out for this team for real and didn't make it. He probably rub it in my face and give me I told you so." ROGER tells Matt, "I didn't know that. I don't think the manager invited you to spend a day here with us and work out with a team. If there was a contest for a millionth fan, he would've told all of us." MATT tells Roger, "Maybe he forgot." Two players finished the one-hundred yard mark and the coach sees Matt and Roger next for their mark. YANKEES COACH tells them, "Schultz, Rajesh. Come on, you're up." Roger sees the Yankees coach and tells Matt were next. ROGER tells Matt, "Come on, Matt. Were next." MATT tells Roger, "What are we doing?" ROGER tells Matt, "The hundred yard dash, to see how fast we are!" MATT tells himself, "I don't know, if I still have the running power. One way to find out." Matt and Roger take their position in the hundred yard dash and the Yankees coach blows the whistle. Matt and Roger starts running. Matt tries to catch up, but can't do it. But Matt stops thinking and starts running fast as he could and beats Roger in the hundred yard dash. Yankees Coach whistles and stops. Jeff goes over to the Yankees coach and checks out Matt's speed. YANKEES COACH tells Matt, "Skipper, check this out." Jeff looks at the stop watch at Matt for a minute. JEFF tells the Yankees Coach, "Six point seven seconds. That's amazing, that kid can fly. Let's see how good he is in batting." Riley is on the mound, waiting to pitch his game Batting cage. Jeff enters the batting cage and sees Riley. Riley was shocked to see his father. Riley tells his Dad, "Dad, what are you doing here? Jeff tells Riley, "I'm the new manager." Riley tells his Dad, "Manager of what? Jeff tells Riley, "The Yankees." Riley tells Jeff, "How did you get this job?" Riley tells Jeff, "George Jackson, the new GM hired me right away right after I got laid off from architecture job." Riley tells Jeff, "I'm really sorry about that Dad. Dad do you think have any coaching experience, I hardly doubt coached a baseball team?" Jeff tells Riley, "I did a coach a team and I took them to a championship team. Riley figured out and tells Jeff, "That was a little league team that your architecture firm sponsored. But they still hired you as a manager with no less coaching experience." Jeff tells Riley, "Even I didn't believe it first, but since George called me. I took the job and don't worry you won't get any special treatment since I'm the manager. I have to treat you like every other player." Riley tells Jeff, "That what I was afraid of. Please I really need to be back in this team, my life depends on your decision." Jeff tells Riley, "We'll see how good you are during the cuts and see if you are good enough you are to make this team." Riley tells Jeff,

"My future is in the hands of my father. That's what I was afraid of." Jeff tells Riley, "All right Mikey, go warm up you ready to pitch." Riley tells Jeff, "I definitely need a miracle to make this team?" Yankees catcher is on the plate waiting for Riley to pitch. Jeff watches Riley pitching. Riley is ready for the ball and starts pitching really mediocre. The ball hit's the mitt and one of the coaches next to Jeff who's carrying a radar gun for a minute. JEFF tells the Yankees Coach 2, "How far?" YANKEES COACH 2 tells Jeff, "Eighty-two!" JEFF tells Riley, "Come on, Riley hit It.? Riley throws the ball mediocre again, misses the catcher and the batting cage. Jeff looks at the coach for a minute. YANKEES COACH 2 tells Jeff, "Still Eighty-two!" JEFF tells Riley, "I know Riley, still has the power like he used to have. I know he could do it. Hey Riley, I know you could do it, come on give it to me!" Riley sees Jeff outside the batting cage for a minute. RILEY tells Jeff, "Jeff! If he said, I could do it! I could do it!" Riley stops thinking throws the ball really hard and hit's the catcher's mitt really hard. YANKEE'S CATCHER tells Jeff, "Man, that stings!" Yankee's catcher takes the ball out and the coach sees the target speed on his radar gun. YANKEES COACH 2 tells Jeff, "You never going to guess, how fast that went!" JEFF tells Yankees Coach 2, "How fast?" Yankees Coach 2 sees the speed on the radar gun to Jeff for a minute.

JEFF tells Yankees Coach 2, "101, I can't believe it." Riley throws the pitch two more times and hit's the catcher's mitt. Yankee's Catcher hand still stings when he takes out the ball. Yankees Coach 2 tells Jeff the next speed on the radar gun. YANKEES COACH 2 tells Jeff, "103!" JEFF tells Yankees Coach 2 "Riley still has the heat, why did this team, send him back to the minors." Riley throws another pitcher, but this time it's another heater and it hit's the batting cage missing the catcher's mitt. Riley throws the balls five more times, still hit's the batting cage and not the catcher's mitt. JEFF tells Yankees Coach 2, "I can see, why he was sent back to the minors. He still has the heat, but he can't throw the ball to the catcher's mitt and he's always missing it." YANKEES COACH 2 tells Jeff, "What made him, miss those?" JEFF tells Yankees Coach 2 "I think he's losing his focus. I think I better help him with that." David is in the centerfield, trying to catch the ball and misses it. The batter throws another ball, David tries to catch it near the center wall and misses it and bumps into the centerfield wall and falls down on the grass where the ball is on the grass. Matt is up to bat on home plate and Jeff is watching him bat. The pitcher throws the ball, Matt hit's the ball between second and third base. The pitcher throws the ball, Matt hit's the ball in the left field lane. The pitcher throws the ball, Matt hit's the ball and goes near the pitcher's mound. The pitcher throws the ball, Matt hit's it when an infield fly and drops it near the pitcher's mound for a few seconds. The pitcher throws the ball, Matt's hits it again, hit's the cage and the ball comes down on Matt's batting helmet. Matt falls down on the floor, gets up from the floor and Jeff goes over to Matt and talk to him. JEFF tells Matt, "Listen Schultz, you may run like Carl Lewis and you hit like a five year old girl. A couple of those hits I saw in the beginning almost like you can run threw three bases or inside the park homerun. I think you should leg him out and get on base." MATT tells Jeff, "You want me to get on a base or hit a inside the park home run." JEFF tells Jeff, "If you want to make this team, Matt." MATT tells Jeff, "Make this team, I didn't come here to try out. I thought I was just a millionth fan to spend a day spring training and work out with the players here. It sounded like I was trying out for the team for real." JEFF tells Matt, "A millionth fan, funny Matt. Funny. You know I didn't invite you here in this park, to spend a day here and work out with this team. You here to try out for this team, to see if you're good enough to make it in the majors. From all the cuts." MATT tells Jeff, "Cuts, if I got red tagged. I would be sent to the minors." JEFF tells Matt, "You betcha, a contest. You are one funny guy, Matt." MATT tells Jeff, "Refresh my memory. What was my first name here, before I came to this camp? JEFF tells Matt, "Axel, that was your name on the list. When you told me it was Matt, I always thought Axel was your nickname or something." Matt is totally shocked, that he is trying out for the major leagues and he knows there's no contest here and he was invited here by accident. But as somebody else who was supposed to be invited here, not Matt. MATT tells Jeff,

"I think their's a big misundersta…?" Matt stops for a minute and think this might be a good thing. JEFF tells Matt, "Matt, what were you going to say?" MATT tells Jeff, "Oh, Axel is my nickname. How silly of me, but just call me Matt anyway, if you guys want me to answer." JEFF tells Matt, "Okay, Matt." MATT tells Jeff, "There is a couple of questions I want to ask, before I start batting again?" JEFF tells Matt, "Go ahead!" MATT tells Jeff, "What minor league team, did I play for? Before I was invited here and what is my salary if I make the team." JEFF tells Matt, "I don't know what the salary is right now, if you do make the team. You probably make three hundred thousand to start and you played Clearwater Threshers, the Philadelphia Phillies farm team you played for six years right after you got drafted after high school when you were eighteen." MATT tells Jeff, "Well, I was just checking for a minute. I just lost my head." JEFF tells Matt, "Okay, Matt. Remember leg them out. If you hit another infield fly and miss the ball. You will have to do ten pushups. Is that understood, Matt?" MATT tells Jeff, "Yes skipper." JEFF tells Matt, "Good, glad we understand each other." Jeff exit's the batting cage, Matt is back on the plate and the pitchers throws the ball. Matt swings the ball and gets a strike. Jeff looks at Matt for a minute. JEFF tells Matt, "You know the drill, Matt." MATT tells Jeff, "I know, I know. I have to do ten pushups, if I miss the ball or hit an infield fly." Matt puts his bat down and starts doing his ten pushups. Roger is on the home plate, the pitcher throws the ball slowly and Roger hit's the ball and the ball goes over the fence centerfield wall. The Pitcher throws the ball really slow and Roger hits it and goes over left field wall. The pitcher throws the ball again really slow, Roger hit's the ball and hits over the centerfield wall again. Jeff looks at Roger batting for a minute with Yankees Coach 2 and really impressed about his hitting. JEFF tells Yankees Coach 2, "This kid is a good power hitter, how come the club hasn't called him up." The pitcher throws the ball really fast, Roger swings his bat and misses it. That was a strike. The pitcher throws the ball really fast again, Roger swings his bat and misses it. The pitcher throws the ball really fast again, Roger swings his bat and misses it again. Jeff looks at Roger for a minute. JEFF tells the Yankees Coach 2, "Now I know, why he wasn't called up. He can hit the ball hard by a slow ball, but he can't hit fastball. I have to help him with the fastball. This going to be a long spring training." The Yankee players and Matt and Riley enter the locker room right now head to their lockers. MATT tells Riley, "I'm kind of scared to open it right now." RILEY tells Matt, "Relax, Matt. They're not going to cut anybody on the first day." MATT tells Riley, "If you insist Riley." Matt opens his locker and there is no red tag. Matt is relieved for a minute. MATT tells Riley, "Thank god." RILEY tells Matt, "Don't get cocky, kid. We have a long way to go." Roger is practicing his batting skills, he gets another strike from another fastball in the batting cage. Riley throws another fast pitch and hit's the catcher's head. Riley throws another pitch and hit's the batting cage wall. Matt hit's the ball for an infield fly and that doesn't look good for Jeff. Matt does ten pushups. David hit's the centerfield wall trying to catch the ball again. A pop fly, David tries to catch it and misses it. David and the other Yankee's tries to catch the ball and hits David in the head. David falls down on the floor. Yankees pitcher throws the pitch. Matt swings the bat and hit's the ball for an infield fly in the baseball field. Matt looks at Jeff for a minute, Matt starts doing his ten pushups. Riley throws the pitch and hit's the Boston Red Sox batter in batting helmet. Riley throws another pitch, Los Angeles Dodgers batters hit's the ball and it's out of the park for a homerun. Matt swings the bat, hit's the ball and tries to run all four bases for an inside the park homerun and tries to slide when the left fielder grab the ball on the grass and throws it to the catcher and gets Matt out when he tries to reach home. David goes to his locker room, starts praying to god that he doesn't get red tagged and he opens his locker room and doesn't have one. Matt opens his locker and sees there is no red tag. David tries to catch the ball and hit's the centerfield wall again when he misses the catch in the baseball field. Roger swings the bat and gets struck out again by a fastball. Matt tries to dive for the ball and misses it when the ball goes leftfield. Riley throws another pitch and hit's the wall near the catcher and the umpire and misses it. Riley throws another pitch, the catcher misses the ball when the ball hit's the wall again and the umpire tells the Seattle Mariner's batter to take his base. Roger swings the bat again, gets strike out again. Matt swings his bat, hit's the near second and third base, but the Twins shortstop grabs the ball and Matt slides on first and the shortstop throws to the first baseman. First Baseman caught the ball and tags out Matt. Matt looks at his locker in the locker room, to see if makes another cut this week. MATT tells himself, "If I get cut again, I'm going to jump off this roof. The way I played, I think they'll cut me right now." Matt opens his locker and no red tag. MATT tells Riley, "I made it and more to go." Matt cell phone rings on his locker for a minute, Matt gets his cell phone out and answers it. MATT answers the cell phone and ask, "Hello!" GARY'S VOICE tells Matt, "Hey Matt, where did you go? We were in the hotel and the hotel clerk told me you haven't checked in yet?" MATT tells Gary on his cell phone, "What about you guys, I've been trying to call you guys for a week. Where did you guys go?" GARY'S VOICE tells Matt, "We were partying in Daytona. We meet an heiress and her friend in Spring Break, we hit it off and they invited us to spend a week in the Bahamas We were so wasted, got drunk in the limo and hop on their private jet that send us to the Bahamas. When we woke up, in a luxurious hotel and we met the girls we decided to spend a week here. After the week was over, we came back to Tampa and here we are." MATT tells Gary, "That explains, why I couldn't call you guys. And you guys didn't see me in the stands." GARY'S VOICE tells Matt, "What are you talking about and where are you anyway. Me and Rick are about to check out and wait for you. So, we can go home." MATT tells Gary, "You and Rick, will have go home without me." GARY'S VOICE tells Matt, "How come and where are you?" MATT tells Gary, "You won't believe me if I told you. For a couple months, if I make this team." GARY'S VOICE tells Matt, "What team are you talking about? The only team I know in Tampa is….?" Gary figured it out where Matt is at? GARY'S VOICE tells Matt, "No way are you in…?" Matt interrupts Gary for a minute. MATT tells Gary, "I know, I'll explain, later when I get back from New York." GARY'S VOICE tells Matt, "I don't get it, how on earth did they let you in Spring Training and let you try out for this team." MATT tells Gary, "Like I said, I'll explain later." GARY'S VOICE tells Matt, "Man, I got to tell Rick. He's going to freak when he finds out where you are?" MATT tells Rick, "Just tell Rick, not to tell anyone else where I am. I think I can get a lot of trouble for doing this." GARY'S VOICE tells Matt, "How much trouble?" MATT tells Gary, "A lot of trouble." GARY'S VOICE that he is frightened and tells Matt, "That bad, huh. Don't worry, your secret is safe with me and so is Rick. When you get back, can you explain to me what's going on?" MATT tells Gary, "Sure, no problemo." GARY'S VOICE tells Matt, "What about the library, whose going to cover for you?" MATT tells Gary, "I'll let the new girl Ashley cover for me.

She used to be in charge of her library in college. I think she can handle this library, she has experience. That's what Rick told me about her in the airplane when I want to know more about her from Rick?" GARY'S VOICE tells Matt, "What are you going to tell her where you are, for the next few months?" MATT tells Gary, "I'll tell her, I'm house sitting for my cousin in Tampa in a few months. I think she'll buy that." GARY'S VOICE tells Matt, "Well good luck with that." MATT tells Gary, "Bye Gary!" GARY'S VOICE tells Matt, "See ya, Matt!" Matt hangs up his phone. MATT tells himself, "This is going to be a long Spring Training." Back in the baseball field. Riley throws another wild pitch, hit's a Anaheim Angels batter in the batting helmet and he takes his base. David tries to make the catch, but the ball hits his head and goes over the fence for a homerun. Roger swings his bat and gets struck out again. Matt slides to home plate and Toronto Blue Jays Catcher tags him out when he tries to get on base. Riley throws another pitch, the Yankees catcher couldn't get the ball when it hit's the wall and misses it. Riley throws another pitch and the batter hits it and the ball hits Riley in the forehead. Riley gets upset and punches the batter out and they start to fight. The Umpires and the players break them up. Riley, Matt, Roger and David enter the locker room for final cut day and stop for a minute. RILEY tells them, "What day is it, today? Because I've been practicing all my pitches that would end up in blooper reel for sports illustrated and worrying about my future if I see a red tag for the last few months." ROGER tells them, "I already checked the calendar, but I don't think you would like what day it is?" MATT tells Roger, "Were already here, Roger. Just tell us anyway?" ROGER tells them, "Final cut down day." DAVID tells them, "I was afraid of that. I've been shunned from my community and my family to play here. If I see that red tag, this will be worse than been shunned from my community. I feel like I'm being shunned here too." ROGER tells David, "We've been playing badly for the last few months and our record 2 and 18. That means we were in dead last in spring training. The way we played, we'll be sent back to the minors." DAVID tells them, "Being sent back to the minors, is a lot worse for your entire family and your church that ignores you for playing this game. Sometimes, I wanted to know if I made the right decision leaving the community to play here." MATT tells David, "Were about to find out David?" RILEY tells them, "Who wants to go first?" DAVID tells Roger, "I'll go, even though my dad prayed to god that I rot in hell for leaving for the community to play here. God will probably tell my father that he I was sent back to the minors, he'll probably rub it in. For leaving the order and I even pray to god, that I want to be here. I hate to say, god chooses." ROGER tells David, "It won't be god, it will be Jeff that decide if we stay or leave?" DAVID tells Roger, "Jeff already is playing god, well here goes." David heads to his locker, prays to god that he doesn't get a red tag and opens it. David looks at his locker and there is no red tag. DAVID tells them, "No red tag, I'm in the majors. I'm a Yankee. I'm going to New York. I'm going to my pal in the general store and tell him to tell my dad I'm playing for the Yankees. Man, will this piss him off. I'm going to call him" RILEY tells David, "I thought the community shunned you for coming here." DAVID tells Riley, "He's an Englishman and plus the guy works in Hy-Vee. Whose a friend of my family, I think he should tell my father." RILEY tells David, "Well good luck." David sees the land phone in the locker room, goes over there and calls his friend from the general store. Riley looks at Roger for a minute. RILEY tells Roger, "Well, Roger. It's your turn." ROGER tells Riley, "Okay, if I don't make this team. I probably will have go back and work in my father's practice. Which, I don't want to do that. If I do make this team, I tell him and he will cut me off and won't speak to me in a million years. Well here goes." Roger goes to his locker and opens his locker. Roger looks at his locker and sees no red tag in his locker. ROGER tells himself, "No red tag, I'm made the team. I'm a Yankee, I'm a Yankee. Man, I want to call my father and tell him to take his job and shove it in his face. That will be too good for him. I'll just tell him, I'm playing for the Yankees and yell at me in hindi. But, it will be worth it. Good luck, Riley, Matt." MATT tells Roger, "Well, I'm going to need it Rog." Roger heads to his phone and wait for his turn since David is on the phone. Riley looks at Matt for a minute. RILEY tells Matt, "Well Matt, it's your turn." MATT tells Riley, "Wish me luck, I'm going to need it." Matt heads to his locker, opens his locker and closes his eyes for a minute. Matt opens his eyes and sees there is no red tag.

MATT tells Riley, "I made the team, I'm a Yankee. I'm a Yankee! I'm going to call Gary and tell him." RILEY tells Matt, "Whose Gary!" MATT tells Riley, "My friend from New York, I'm going to tell him the good news." Matt heads to the phone and wait for his turn to call Rick and Gary. Riley looks at his locker for a minute. RILEY tells himself, "I guess this is my turn, if David, Matt and Roger can make it. Maybe I can too." Riley heads to his locker and opens it for a minute. Riley sees a red tag and he's really angry and hurt for a minute. Riley punches the locker with his fist. Jeff is working in his office, until he hears a door knock and stops working for a minute. JEFF ask who it is, "Come in." Riley opens the door with a baseball on his right hand and closes the door really hard. RILEY tells Jeff, "My own father, You haven't seen the last of me Pop. I can't believe I played with you back in the minors. You and I were used to be great friends. What is this, were you jealous of me that I made it to the majors and you didn't. I used to be a superstar athlete with a multimillion dollar endorsement contract, that I'm going to lose all that, my house and your granddaughter will have go to a community college. Because my agent told me, if I don't get back in the majors. I could lose it all. You know why, because my endorsement contract and my Pepsi distributorship was my income to pay for my house and my daughter's college. Now, I'm going to be sent back to the minors again and lose it all. Thanks to you, you heartless asshole. You put your own son and your granddaughter will be out in the street because of you. Don't you worry, I'll get another shot. When I do, I'm going to pitch the ball right in your face. Like this!" Riley throws the ball really hard and hit's the locker. RILEY tells his Dad, "And this, when I see you again!" Riley sees the baseball and throws it in his father's face. Jeff's nose hurts and covers it for a minute, but it does not hurt. RILEY tells his Dad, "You know, Dad. I'm maybe wil be sent back to the minors, but you know what. There will be another major league will take me and you can take this team and shove it. I'm out of here." Riley is about to exit for a minute, Jeff examines his nose and he's fine. Jeff sits back down in his chair and starts applauding. JEFF tells Riley, "I love that performance, it's got academy award written all over it." Riley stops for a minute and turns around and head to Jeff's desk. Riley stops for a minute. JEFF tells Riley, "I like that in a new player and my new team captain." RILEY tells Jeff, "I beg your pardon." JEFF tells his Son, "Michael, I never cut you. I was looking for a new team leader, I picked you. I need to test you to see if you care about playing here and your teammates. You passed, congratulations Riley. You're my new captain." RILEY tells Jeff, "I passed, you were never going to cut me." JEFF tells Riley, "Of course, Mike I was with you in the stands when you played in the minors. I always knew you had some potential in you. I think you still do, I wanted to see if you still have the heart to play the game. You still do. Congratulations, Captain." RILEY tells Jeff, "Thanks Dad. I'm really sorry throwing the ball in your face. I was way out of line." JEFF tells Riley, "I would've done the same thing, in your same situation. Come on, we better pack up." RILEY tells Jeff, "Where?" JEFF tells Riley, "New York City, were going home tomorrow. Welcome back, Riley!" RILEY tells Riley, "You too, Pop." Jeff gets up from his chair and goes over to Jeff and starts hugging him for a minute. Matt is on the phone with Gary for a minute in the locker room. MATT tells Gary on the phone, "Bye Gary, I'll see you tomorrow." Matt hangs up the phone for a minute. Riley sees Matt, David and Roger for a minute and goes over talk to them. MATT tells Riley, "Hey Riley, I'm really sorry." ROGER tells Riley, "Me too." RILEY tells them, "Thanks guys, I appreciate that. I'm going to pack my bags for a minute." DAVID tells Riley, "Back to the minors." RILEY tells them, "Yeah, in New York City." MATT tells Riley, "New York City, I thought they red tagged you." RILEY tells them, "Misunderstanding, it was a practically joke on my Dad. I'm your new captain off this team." DAVID tells Riley, "Welcome aboard captain." Matt, David and Roger salute to Riley for a minute. The airplane landed on the runway and headed to New York LaGuardia airport. Matt and Riley exit's the dugout box outside Yankees Stadium and head to the field for a minute. MATT tells Riley, "When I was a kid, my mom took me out here once. She had season tickets for the red sox, it was an away game and when we stopped in Yankees Stadium. When I saw the players in playing in that stadium. It was like magic." RILEY tells Matt, "That's what I remembered when I first came out here. I wanted to have that magic again." MATT tells Riley, "What happened to that magic anyway?" RILEY tells Matt, "The magic lost its fuel, I always keep thinking where the service station is at so I can fill it up again." MATT tells Riley, "How long it's been since you haven't played out here in this field?" RILEY tells Matt, "A long time." Matt looks at Riley for a minute. RILEY tells Matt, "A long time." MATT tells Riley, "I bet you twenty bucks you couldn't get me out." RILEY tells Matt, "Will see about that?" Matt and Riley head to the dugout to grab Riley's baseball glove and Matt's bat. Riley throws the ball in the mound and Matt swings away and gets a strike in home plate. RILEY tells Matt, "Strike One!" MATT tells Riley, "It wasn't a ball, it didn't go over the plate." RILEY tells Matt, "Trust me, it was a strike." MATT tells Riley, "All right, I'll call it a strike. I bet you can't throw it again". RILEY tells Matt, "Well see about that." Riley throws the ball and Matt hit's the ball near the centerfield wall. RILEY tells Matt, "Practically, impressive Matt. That's looks like an inside the park home run." MATT tells Riley, "Well, there is another hit I want to show you. But I don't know, if you're man enough to throw it." RILEY tells Matt, "Well, I'm man enough to throw it. Let's see this hit." MATT tells Riley, "Well, I haven't hit this since the cape league championship. Lay it on me, Riles!" RILEY tells Matt, "You ask for it?" Riley throws the ball and Matt sees the ball. Matt hit's the ball for an infield fly. Matt runs through the bases and Riley tries to catch the ball. Matt runs through the bases slowly and Riley tries to dive for the ball and misses it. Matt runs through the home plate when his foot touches home plate. The baseball falls down on the grass where Riley misses the ball. Riley gets up from the floor from the grass for a minute and goes over talk to Riley. RILEY tells Matt, "Wow that was an infield fly homerun. I haven't see anyone do that, except Babe Ruth. How come you never hit that infield fly homerun in spring training? " MATT tells Riley, "Because, I can only do it only once. It almost cost me a shot in the….?" Matt looks at Riley for a minute. MATT tells Riley, "Nearly cost me a shot in the majors. When I blew my knee out." RILEY tells Matt, "That explains, why you can't run a lot faster. But if you don't slide through home plate, maybe you won't blew your knee out if you do it again." MATT tells Riley, "Well, I'll think about it." RILEY tells Matt, "Come on, we better head home. We have a first game tomorrow." MATT tells Riley, "Wish us luck, we have a long way to go." RILEY tells Matt, "Yeah, were going to need it." Riley sees the baseball, throws it in the sky and falls down from the sky. The game just started, that is not a sellout crowd and the ball hit's the glove where Riley is wearing. YANKEE'S BROADCASTERS tells the fans, "Hello Baseball fans, welcome to Yankees Stadium, I'm Ray Sterling the voice of the Yankees." RAY STERLING the Yankees Broadcaster who is about in his late thirties and his broadcasting partner AL WENTZ who's in early twenties whose a nerdy sidekick in his broadcasting booth.

RAY tells the fans, "My broadcasting partner Al Wentz." AL tells Ray, "Today is opening day for the Yankees Ray." RAY tells Al, "You betcha, Al. For two year losing streak we have a new lineup and a new manager getting us out of the gutter." AL tells the fans, "You got that one right, Ray. Here's our new manager of the Yankees Jeff Riley?" Jeff Riley gets out of the dugout box and people barely clap him in the baseball field. RAY'S VOICE tells the fans, "Yeah, our very own Yankees fans are giving a warm welcome to our new manager. Or I think." AL'S VOICE tells the fans, "The Yankees will be facing off the Defending American League champs Texas Rangers. Left Fielder Ashton Klux is up first." Ashton Klux is on the home plate and carrying a bat in his left hand near the mound and gets ready to bat. Riley carries a rosin bag to wash his hands and puts it down on the pitcher's mound. AL'S VOICE tells the fans, "Starting pitcher for the Yankees is our very own long awaiting the veteran Mike Riley. How about that Jeff Riley former superstar son playing together as fan and son. Riley's kid is an eight time all-star and nominated for cy young eight times. After being sent back to the minors for two years ago." Ray and Al are doing the play-by-play in the broadcasting booth. Ray is drinking his bottle of bud light and Al is eating his hot dog. AL tells the fans, "It has something do fighting with the umpire and his manager. He had a few suspensions and fines that might send back to the minors. Since his pitching wasn't the same." RAY tells his fans, "Even though they were just rumors, Riley's pitching wasn't the same two years ago. He hasn't got out of his slump back in the minors." Riley is on the mound, sees Klux on home plate ready to bat. He's batting right area of home plate in the baseball field. The catcher gives Riley a signal that he's ready. RAY'S VOICE tells the fans, "The catcher's gives Riley a signal, Riley nods his head and likes the sign. Riley throws the first pitch." Riley throws the first pitch and it's way off side and catcher misses the ball. The Umpire makes the call. HOME PLATE UMPIRE tells the batter, "Ball 1!" RAY'S VOICE tells the fans, "Ball 1." Yankees catcher grabs the ball, throws it back to Riley and Riley catches the ball on his glove. Riley throws the ball again for another and the catcher misses the ball again when it hit's the grass. RAY'S VOICE tells the fans, "Ball 2!" Riley throws the ball again and the catcher misses the ball again on his glove. RAY'S VOICE tells the fans, "Ball 3!" Riley throws the ball again and the catcher misses the ball again on his glove and hit's the grass. RAY'S VOICE tells the fans, "Ball 4!" The umpire tells Ashton take his base. Ashton gives the bat to the bat boy and heads to first base. Riley throws the ball to the next batter and the catcher misses it again. RAY'S VOICE tells the fans, "Ball 1!" Riley throws the ball to the next batter and the catcher misses it again. RAY'S VOICE tells the fans, "Ball 2!" Riley throws the ball to the next batter two times and the catcher misses it again. RAY'S VOICE tells the fans, "Ball 4!" The next Texas Ranger's batter exit's the dugout and heads to home plate. RAY'S VOICE tells the fans, "Rick Lavene, Last year's home run leader, AL MVP and six time all-star is up. He batted over 600 when he was facing Riley two years ago. These two guys were old rivals." Lavene sees Riley on the mound. Lavene is on the home plate and ready to bat. LAVENE tells Riley, "Riley, is that you? I thought you were still in the minors?" RILEY tells Lavene, "I got called right back up." LAVENE tells Riley, "I always loved humiliating you, watching my career sky rocket and your career down the toilet. Too bad they should've released you." RILEY "Not today, I'll give you my wild pitch to prove that my career is about to launch and your career just been scrubbed." LAVENE tells Riley, "Bring it on, has beened!" Riley throws the pitch hard and Lavene hit's the ball out of the park centerfield line. Lavene drops his bat and starts running through bases and Riley is humiliated again. Lavene runs through home plate for a minute. LAVENE tells Riley, "Don't quit your day job, Riley!" Riley throws the ball to another Rangers batter, the batter hits it and the ball hits near second and third base where Matt is the shortstop dives down on the ground to catch the ball but misses it. That gives another Rangers batter run two bases. The next Rangers batter hit's the ball and David catches the ball in centerfield that ends the first inning. Ray and Al are doing the play-by-play in the broadcasting booth. RAY tells the fans, "Well Al, after Riley comeback where he gives away two runs and a homer off his former rival. The Ranger are leading 3 to 0 and rangers are on the lead." Matt is up to bat and the Rangers pitcher is on the mound in the baseball field. Matt is on home plate and ready to bat. AL'S VOICE tells the fans, "The Yankees are down by three and they need to get something going?" RAY'S VOICE tells the fans, "Newcomer Matt Schultz is up to bat, this new kid hasn't done really good in spring training. His batting average was ninty in spring training and made twenty errors. But our new manager Riley, this kid has good potential for something going. Let's see what he's got." The Rangers pitcher throws the ball, Matt hit's the near right field. Where two Rangers Outfielders trying to catch the ball and misses it. Matt drops his bat and runs three bases. Rangers right fielder got the ball throws it to third. RAY'S VOICE tells his fans, "Schultz, hits it right deep right and Young and Nutz going after the fly ball but misses it. Young got the ball and throws it to third." Young throws the ball to third, but Matt makes it to third base right on time and the third base umpire yells safe. AL'S VOICE tells the fans, "And Schultz made it in just in time."

Ryan, George and REYNOLDS are in the Owners box and sitting down watching the game. REYNOLDS tells Ryan, "You know Ryan, thanks for inviting me to the game. I appreciate that." RYAN tells Reynolds, "Thanks, I appreciate that Dalton." REYNOLDS tells them, "It's going to be great, you'll be losing this bet and this team will be all mine. When I turn this stadium into condominiums and watch this team go down in dirt. Since this team you invited to spring training, went 2 and 18. I think I have this team in the bag." GEORGE tells Reynolds, "Game's not over Reynolds. We just started." REYNOLDS tells Ryan, "These losers that your new manager picked out of that lineup are a joke. Just like this team and the other players who played in this team before." RYAN tells Reynolds, "So, why do you hate the Yankees in the first place?" REYNOLDS tells them, "These losers that Colonel Rupert picked out back then were all jokes. Like Babe Ruth, Lou Gehrig, Roger Maris and Mickey Mantle were all jokes. Those guys weren't players, they were a circus act that should be seen in a freak show. These freaks you have now, belong in the circus and so does the new manager of yours. That's the reason, why I'm a Rangers fan. Those are players who have dicks and they're real man. Not these court jesters you have in this field." GEORGE tells Reynolds, "You know Reynolds, I would love to beat the snot out of you for that. But I'm not, because I'm not you. But one thing, I wanted to ask?" REYNOLDS tells George, "Lay it on me, Georgie?"

GEORGE tells Reynolds, "Why did you buy this team in the first place. Why didn't you buy the Rangers in the first place, since you hate the Yankees?" REYNOLDS tells them, "If I buy the Rangers, then I have to look at those ugly Yankees uniforms and those ugly players we have to play for. I want my team to play for the best, so if I buy the team from Green. Tear it down, turn it into condominiums and make a lot of money for it. I can buy my favorite team and not look at their ugly faces and you guys again." RYAN tells Reynolds, "We'll see about that. Come on, Schultz. I know you can do it." Back in the baseball field. Matt is on third base with Rangers third baseman and trying to run to home plate. Luis is up to bat and Ranger's pitcher is ready to pitch. RAY'S VOICE tells the fans, "Schultz is on third and Luis is up to bat." Matt is about to steal home for a minute. RANGERS THIRD BASEMAN tells Matt, "Going somewhere dickface?" MATT tells the Ranger's Third Baseman, "Yeah, straight to home. Now excuse me, I'm ready to give out my hall of fame speech at home. See ya dip shit!" Matt steals home and Rangers Third Baseman said something to Matt for a minute when he shouts at something to Matt. RANGERS THIRD BASEMAN tells Matt, "Hey Schultz, flies open!" Matt tries to slide through fourth base, when he heard what the Rangers third baseman said and Matt got distracted when he slides through near fourth base and misses it when the Rangers pitcher throws the ball to his catch and the catcher got it. The Rangers catcher tags out Matt. RAY'S VOICE tells the fans, "Schultz tries to steal home, Denton throws it hard at home and Dryer got it." HOMEPLATE UMPIRE tells Matt, "You're out!" AL'S VOICE tells the fans, "Schultz is out, he was that close to stealing home. Close, but no cigar." Matt lays his head on the dirt. Rangers batter hit's the ball, David is on center field trying to get the ball and the ball hits his head and falls down on the dirt. The next Rangers batter hit's the ball, near first and second base. Matt dives down on the ground to get the ball and got it. Throws the ball to first and misses it. When the first baseman couldn't catch the ball, since Matt throws it the wrong way to right field. The Rangers batter can run through an inside the park homerun. The Rangers batter hit's the ball, both Roger and David tries to catch and they bumped into each other and misses the ball. Roger is up to bat, strikes out when the Rangers hit's a fastball. Riley throws the pitch, but the Yankees catcher misses the ball and the home plate umpire tells the Rangers batter to take his base. Riley throws the ball again and Rangers batter gets hit by a pitch. Matt is up to bat and hit's the ball deep to center and hit's the wall. Matt tries to make an inside the park homerun and the Rangers centerfielder grabs the ball that was on the grass and throws the ball all the way to the Rangers catcher. The catcher caught it and Matt slides through fourth base and misses it for a mile. When the Rangers catcher tags him out. Riley is on the mound and the Lavene is on home plate. RAY'S VOICE tells the fans,

"It's top of the eight, Riley's is on the mound and it's two down. Lavene is up to bat." Lavene is ready to bat and sees Riley for a minute. LAVENE tells Riley, "You're still here, I thought they would've taken you out. Since were up to three." RILEY tells Lavene, "That's going to change when I get you out." LAVENE tells Riley, "Come on, Riley. Let's see what you got. I don't think you still have it." RILEY tells Lavene, "We'll see about that." Riley throws the ball hard and Lavene's got a good read out to the ball. Lavene hit's the ball hard and hits it out of the park in right field. LAVENE tells Riley, "You should gotten back to the minors, Riley. That's where you belong. So, does the rest of your loser team!" RILEY tells Lavene, "You know, Laven I should've threw the ball not in home plate. But I should've threw it in your face. But I think I'll let my fist do that for me!" Riley goes over to the home plate and punches out Lavene. These two guys start brawling. AL'S VOICE tells the fans, "Looks like Riley and Lavene are going to start the championship rematch right now. I think it's the fight of the century." The rest of the team tries to break them up. RAY'S VOICE tells the fans, "Looks like everybody else join in." Jeff sees Riley fighting with Lavene in the dugout. JEFF tells them, "I think it's time, I take Riley out." Riley and Lavene continues fighting. JEFF tells them, "I think I better do it now." The umpire separates Riley and Lavene for a minute when all the players break them up. AL'S VOICE tells the fans, "Well, the ump and the rest of the team separates Riley and Lavene.

Looks like the Ump is going to make a call." HOME PLATE UMPIRE tells Riley, "Riley, you're out of here. Lavene go run through the four bases." Riley is upset about this decision. RILEY tells the Home plate Umpire, "You want to take me out. I'll take you out, you son of a bitch. When I kick your balls in the rear!" HOME PLATE UMPIRE tells Riley, "Out Riley, Out!" RILEY tells Home Plate Umpire, "You can't take me out, you dickshit. I'm leaving. I'm going, you asshole!" Riley leaves the field and the new pitcher goes up the mound. RAY'S VOICE tells the fans, "This is not exactly how Riley, wants to start his comeback. Looks like, he's going to watch the game in the locker room." Riley sees the batting helmets in the dugout and kicks it. Roger is up to bat on home plate and two Yankees players are on second and third base. RAY'S VOICE tells the fans, "It's bottom of the ninth, the Yanks are four runs behind. Two men are second and third and Roger is up to bat. Roger Punjab is the first Indian American to play in the major leagues. Johnson throws the ball." Johnson throws the ball slowly and Roger hit's the ball out of the park in left field. RAY'S VOICE tells the fans, "Punjab hits it deep to left field and it's out of here." Yankees two batters and Roger runs threw home plate to make the score three to four. AL'S VOICE tells the fans, "The Yankees are up to three to four. With two runs behind." The Yankees batter in on third and Matt is on home plate and ready to bat. RAY'S VOICE tells the fans, "Were still two runs behind, we have the tying run on third and Matt is the go head run up to bat." Johnson throws the ball and Matt swings his bat and gets a strike. AL'S VOICE tells the fans, "Johnson throws the ball and Schultz misses. Strike one." Johnson throws the ball again, Matt swings his bat again and gets another strike. AL'S VOICE tells the fans, "Johnson makes another pitch and strike two." RAY'S VOICE tells the fans, "Schultz is 0 and 2. Johnson makes another pitch." Johnson throws the ball and Matt hit's the ball hard and the bat cracks when the ball goes near second and third. Matt runs through three bases. RAY'S VOICE tells the fans, "Schultz hits it near second and third. Rameriz runs through home plate." Rangers shortstop dives down and got the ball. Matt slides through third base and Rangers shortstop threws it to third base and the third baseman got it. AL'S VOICE tells the fans, "Jenz got it and throws it to third. Schultz slides to third." Matt tries to slide third and misses for a minute. Third baseman tags him out. RAY'S VOICE tells the fans, "Misses it by a mile and he's out." The third base umpire makes a decision right now. THIRD BASE UMPIRE tells the fans, "Too late, Schultz didn't make it to third and runner doesn't score. Ball game over!" The Yankees fans are disappointed and so is Jeff. Ray and Al are doing the play-by-play in the broadcasting booth. RAY tells the fans, "Schultz tried to make it third, misses it by a mile. The Rangers won it by four to three and this makes Yankees 200 loss this year." Ray is drinking his beer. AL tells the fans "I guess this new team makes the losing streak a lot worse, since they picked up where it's left off by the old team." Reynolds looks at Ryan and George for a minute in the owner's box. REYNOLDS tells them, "I told you this team was a joke. Looks like this team, will be signed, sealed and delivered to me." RYAN tells the fans, "Season, is not over yet Reynolds." REYNOLDS tells the fans, "No your team, just ended. I already see last place written all over it. I can't wait for this team to crash and burn." Reynolds gets up from his chair and goes inside for a minute. Ryan looks at Reynolds for a minute. RYAN tells George, "Man, I like to deck that guy for a minute." Matt is working in his office in the New York Public Library, until he hears a door knock for a minute. MATT tells the person, "Come in!" The door opens and it's Gary and Rick. Gary and Rick enters the office, Rick closes the office. RICK tells Matt, "Hey Matt?" MATT tells them, "Hey guys!" GARY tells Matt, "How are your doin?" MATT tells Gary, "I'm good, man." Rick and Gary sit down in their chairs and talk to Matt about the game yesterday. RICK tells Matt, "We saw the game on tv in Red Sky yesterday. Tough loss, man." MATT tells Gary, "I can't believe I choked in one game. Those guys I played with are worse then me. How did I get into this mess?" GARY tells Matt, "You impersonated an player who was invited to camp." MATT tells Gary, "I thought I was a millionth customer contest, where I can spend the day in Spring Training and work out with the team. I didn't know I was trying out for the team when they accidental thought I was Axel Schultz." RICK tells Matt, "Whose Axel Schultz?" MATT tells them, "He was the player, who was invited to that camp not me. I'm usually scared, that guy would expose me, when they found out I'm not him." GARY tells Matt, "How come you didn't tell Jeff, you're new manager about this misunderstanding?" MATT tells them, "I don't know, I think somewhere down the line. I wanted to be in that camp and play for the major leagues for one time. You knew I blew my knee out in the Cape League Championship." GARY tells Matt, "You told me that story a million times, Matt." MATT tells Gary, "I blew my shot playing for the Red Sox. When I found out when I was trying out for spring training, it felt great to be part of the game that I used to love. I always prayed to god, that I would have one chance to prove that I can play for the Major Leagues for one day. This is my chance." RICK tells Matt, "What would really happened you're not really Axel Schultz. You can get a lot of trouble for impersonating a player." GARY tells Matt, "Yeah, like legal trouble you can go to jail for this." MATT tells Gary, "I know. I knew the risk when I did this, this is my only shot to play in the majors. It was my destiny go to spring training and play for that team." GARY tells Matt, "What would really happened when the real Axel Schultz shows up?" RICK tells Matt, "And he exposes you as a fraud?" MATT tells Gary, "I did some research, he died in a car crash before he arrived in spring training. I don't have to worry about that, but I did tell them to put my name in the lineup instead of Axel Schultz." GARY tells Matt, "That's a relief, just hope the paparazzi doesn't find out about you." MATT tells Gary, "I worry about that, when the time comes. I tell Jeff myself, if somebody in the media tries to blackmail me." GARY tells Matt, "Well, good luck about that." MATT tells Gary, "I don't know what to do about my game, I chocked in opening day. I hardly doubt, I get my running power back before the season is over." GARY tells Matt, "If anyone can do it, you can." MATT tells Gary, "Thanks Gary, I appreciate that." GARY tells Matt, "Hey, no problemo." The telephone rings and Matt picks up the phone and answers it. MATT answers the phone, "Hello, hey Riley. How you doing?" Gary and Rick are looking at Matt for a minute and seeing him talking to his teammate on the phone. MATT tells Riley, "Yeah sure, I like to hang out with you and Jeff tonight. Turner's Steakhouse at seven. I'll be there. Bye Riley." Matt hangs up his phone and talks to Rick and Gary for a minute. GARY tells Matt, "Who was on the phone Matt?" MATT tells them, "Riley, my teammate from the Yankees. Invited me to hang out with him and Jeff at Turner's Steakhouse tonight at seven." RICK tells Matt, "Riley! Mike Riley the famous Yankees Pitcher who was dumped in the minors two years ago wants to hang out with you?" MATT tells them, "You betcha, he's back in the big leagues now and so am I. It'll be so cool to hang out with and Jeff tonight." GARY tells Matt, "Well, I have to head back to the bar." RICK tells Gary, "I have get back to work. Good luck with your lunch with Riley, Matt!" GARY tells Matt, "Me too!" MATT tells them, "I appreciate that guys Bye!" RICK AND GARY tells Matt, "Bye!" Gary and Rick gets up from their chairs and head to the door. Rick opens the door, Rick and Gary exit's the door and Rick closes the door. Matt grabs his Maxim magazine and starts reading it. Riley, Jeff and Matt are sitting down in their chairs eating their steaks and making a toast with their Coors light beer bottle in Turner's Steakhouse. RILEY tells them, "To the Yanks!" MATT tells them, "To the Yanks!" JEFF tells them, "To the Yanks!" Matt, Riley and Jeff puts their beer bottles together, toast and puts their beer bottles down. Riley is eating his steak with A1 steak sauce and Matt is drinking his beer. MATT tells them, "Can you believe this is our first game in the Major league and we lost big with Rangers yesterday in opening day?" JEFF tells them, "Those guys were good and especially Rick Lavene." RILEY tells them, "God, I hate that guy. He's the main reason why I got send back to the minors in the first place." MATT tells Riley, "Is it because he hit a couple of homeruns over your head." RILEY tells Matt, "No, but true. He always rubs my face his success and always tells everybody that I always hit a homerun off my head with my fastballs." JEFF tells Riley, "Look Mike, I was with you cheering you on when you played with you back in the minors. I remember that huge pitch that you threw that got you called up in the majors." RILEY tells Jeff, "I remember that pitch, it was called the M&M pitch." MATT tells Riley, "Yeah, I remember that pitch. That's what everybody called you M&M Mike Riley. They call you M&M you eat an M&M and throw a 101 pitch that strikes out your batters. How come you don't do that anymore?" RILEY tells Matt, "It lost it's zing when I eat one and I can throw eighty-miles per hour. I guess the M&M rocket fuel went out two years ago and still does." MATT tells Riley, "Well, there has to be a reason why you stop taking them." RILEY tells Matt, "I can give you one reason Matt. It lost it's Zing. I still couldn't get my Zing back when I throw hard. Especially when I pitch against Lavene." JEFF tells Riley, "Well the commissioner Selig is fining you five hundred dollars for punching out Lavene. You start another fight it will be another five hundred or a week's suspension." RILEY tells Jeff, "I'm already back in the major leagues I'm already fined five hundred dollars." MATT tells Riley, "I always thought they were rumors that you were fighting against the umpire that got you dumped in the minors." RILEY tells Matt, "Actually, the rumor was wrong. I didn't punch out the umpire. I punched out Lavene that got me dumped back in the minors. Because of his big mouth." MATT tells Riley, "What exactly did he say, that make you want to deck him." RILEY tells Matt, "I don't know it was a long time ago. I don't want talk about it right now. Right now, we have to figure out a way turn this team around." JEFF tells Riley, "We already dead last in spring training. It's going to take a miracle to figure out how to turn this team around." RILEY tells them, "The entire season is on my shoulders. If I get injured for this season, I don't get nothing and I could lose my endorsement deals and my pepsi distribution if we don't turn this team around." MATT tells them, "We have to play better. The only way we can turn this team around. If we look at a couple players that we can work on." JEFF tells them, "I done some scouting on Roger, the kid is a great power hitter but he can't hit the fastball. Yoder has troubles catching fly balls." MATT tells Jeff, "The other two players we have to worry about is us." JEFF tells Matt, "Matt, you're an excellent runner. You can leg them out for three bases and hit an inside the park homerun. But your speed is not enough to get on base or score a run. So we have to work on your running." MATT tells Riley, "Riley you have the greatest pitching power in baseball. But you don't have the control or the pitching power to get a strike out." JEFF tells Riley, "So, we have to work on your pitching. Like eating M&M's again to get you're pitching again." RILEY tells Jeff, "Pop, I lost my pitching power when I ate those M&M's. I still couldn't get my power back when I don't eat them." JEFF tells Riley, "Well you better get your pitching power back or all of us could be released or send back to the minors. If we fail." RILEY tells his father, "I'll try to work on it Dad." JEFF tells Riley, "Okay, that's all I'm asking." RILEY tells Jeff, "If you guys don't mind, I invited Ashley to have dinner with us if it's okay with you." JEFF tells Riley,

"Sure, no problemo. I really glad to see my granddaughter. We haven't seen her since spring break." MATT tells Riley, "How old your daughter?" RILEY tells Matt, "She's eighteen and attending NYU. She's majoring in library and science." Matt sees Ashley entering the steakhouse and is a little nervous seeing her. MATT is whispering to himself, "What is she doing here? She must have a date or something. This place kind of expensive, how did she afford a place like this?" Ashley sees Riley, Jeff and Matt at their table and goes over talk to them. Riley gets up from his chair for a minute and exit's the table. ASHLEY tells Riley, "Hey Dad, Hey Grandpa!" RILEY tells Ashley, "Hey honey!" Riley hugs her daughter for a minute. Matt is really shocked right now. MATT tells Riley, "Ashley is related to you guys. JEFF tells Ashley, "Hey kiddo!" MATT is whispering to himself, "She's very attractive. She doesn't look anything like Riley. I guess the rumor is true, Ashley's father is Mike Riley the star pitcher of the The Runaway Boys. No wondered I didn't figure it out." Riley let's goes of Ashley for a minute, Ashley hugs her grandpa for a minute and lets go. Riley introduces his daughter to Matt. RILEY tells Ashley, "Hey Matt, I like you to meet my daughter Ashley." MATT tells Ashley, "It's a pleasure to meet you Ashley." RILEY tells Ashley, "My new friend and teammate Matt Schultz." MATT tells Ashley, "It's a pleasure to meet you Ashley." ASHLEY tells Matt, "It's a pleasure to meet you Matt. I think I know you, aren't you my new boss in the library." Matt let's goes of

Ashley's hand for a minute. RILEY tells Matt, "Boss?" JEFF tells Matt, "Okay explain." MATT tells them, "I moonlight as a head librarian. My friend Dex Barq going on a summer cruise, he asked me to fill in for him in the New York Public Library for the summer while he's away." ASHLEY tells Matt, "You know Matt, we never actually met. You know I wanted to meet you in the library, but you're always busy." MATT tells Ashley, "Sorry about that, working on a Dewey decimal system, stacking books and organizing the library cards. But, I don't think I can lighten my schedule so we can talk in the library." ASHLEY tells Matt, "Hey, I never knew you played for the Yankees before." MATT tells Ashley, "You never asked me. If I met you, I would've told you." Matt, Riley, Ashley and Jeff sits down in their chairs and Ashley is sitting next to Matt. Matt is a little nervous and Ashley is smiling for a minute for sitting next to him. ASHLEY tells them, "If it's okay with you guys, my roommate Jessica is coming over. If it's okay she has dinner with us." MATT tells Ashley, "Yeah sure, why not." ASHLEY tells Jessica loudly, "Jessica are table is ready." Ashley's roommate JESSICA enters the restaurant and she is the hostess here. Jessica is in her early twenties and a couple years older than Ashley and is very attractive. Jessica goes over to Matt, Riley, Ashley and Jeff table and talk to them. Jessica sees Riley and has a crush on him. So does Riley. Riley starts blushing for a minute. Ashley slaps him on the shoulder for a minute. RILEY tells Ashley, "What

what!" ASHLEY tells Riley, "Dad that's my roommate." RILEY tells Ashley, "Sorry." Ashley sits down in her chair for a minute and sits right next to Riley for a minute. ASHLEY tells Riley, "Dad, this is Jessica Waldorf." Riley shakes Ashley's hand for a minute. ASHLEY tells Riley, "Jessica, this is my father Mike Riley. I told you about?" RILEY tells Jessica, "It's nice to meet you Jessica." JESSICA tells Riley, "It's nice to meet you too. Mr. Riley." RILEY tells Jessica, "You can call me, Riley." JESSICA tells Riley, "Okay, Riley. So, you're thee Mike Riley. The Runaway Boys Pitcher, eight time all-star and nominated for cy young eight times." RILEY tells Jessica, "You betcha." JESSICA tells Riley, "When I was a kid me and my father stayed up all night watching world series 96 game where you struck out six batters against the Braves. It was a great highlight of my light back then. My father is a great fan of yours." RILEY tells Jessica, "Thanks, I appreciate that." JESSICA tells Riley, "I wondered if you could do something for me." Ashley looks embarrassed about this. ASHLEY tells Riley, "Jess, I don't think this is a good time right now." JESSICA tells Riley, "Well, it's definitely a good time." RILEY tells Jessica, "What is it you want to do for me, Jessica?" Jessica takes out a baseball and pen out of her purse and gives it to Riley. Riley grabs the pen and baseball and observes it for a minute. JESSICA tells Riley, "I wondered if you could sign this ball for my father and mostly me." RILEY tells Jessica, "Sure, I'll be happy too." Riley signs her baseball and it's done. JESSICA tells Riley, "Thanks, my father appreciate for signing his baseball and so do I." RILEY tells Jessica, "I appreciate that, Jessica." JESSICA tells Riley, "You know there were rumors in newspaper, a lot of people you were dead for the last two years?" RILEY tells Jessica, "You can't believe everything in media. I was dumped in the minors for the last two years. My game hasn't been the same ever since." JESSICA tells Riley, "I read, you're back in New York and playing for the Yankees again." RILEY tells Jessica, "Well, I'm back in the majors. But my game hasn't performed well as it used to." JESSICA tells Riley, "I saw the game, you're pitching style isn't good what it used to be. Even, I even seen you fighting against Lavene. He must have pissed you off somehow. But I knew he started the fight, not you." RILEY tells Jessica, "Thanks Jessica, I appreciate that. Just some bad blood between us." Jessica looks at Riley and sees how attracted she is to him. JESSICA tells Ashley, "Riley, I wanted to ask. Is there a Mrs. Riley?" ASHLEY tells Jessica, "Jess!" RILEY tells Ashley, "Hey it's okay. Well Jess, if Ashley told you. I'm Widowed. Ashley's mom died two years ago." JESSICA tells Riley, "Hey, I'm sorry about that. My dad died last year before my senior year." RILEY tells Jessica, "Hey, I'm really sorry about that." JESSICA tells Riley, "Hey, it's okay. It was a long time ago." Jessica touches Riley's leg for a minute. RILEY tells Jessica, "Anyway, since I'm back in the big leagues. This is my new manager Jeff…?" Jessica interrupts Riley for a minute. JESSICA tells Jeff, "I know who you are, you're Jeff Riley. The father of Mike Riley and the new manager of the Yankees. You took your team in Junior College World Series and got drafted for the Yankees. Played in the minors. You blew your knee out while trying to make a triple in the minors and cost him a shot in the majors. You went back to school and got your architecture degree and work in a top architecture firm, in Princeton New Jersey. You coached a little league team that the firm sponsors and you took that team to a little league championship." JEFF tells Jessica, "You got that right, how did you know that Jessica?" JESSICA tells Jeff, "Your bio was in the paper." RILEY tells Jessica, "Anyway this is my new teammate for the Yankees and my best friend Matt Sc…?" Jessica interrupts Riley for a minute. JESSICA tells Matt, "Matt Schultz, got drafted by the Philadelphia Phillies and played for the Clearwater Threshers, the Philadelphia Phillies farm team you played for the last six years. You were a shortstop for that team and not really that good. You haven't got a hit for the last six years. It's one of the main reasons, you weren't called up." RILEY tells Jessica, "You got that right." JESSICA tells Matt, "You know Matt, you look like that kid who played in the College World Series 2008 and was league MVP when his team won. You know you guys have the same name." MATT tells Jessica, "Thanks Jessica, I get that a lot." JESSICA tells them, "I saw the game on tv, you hit a triple in your first game up to bat. But you were out in fourth. I'm really sorry about that." MATT tells

Jeff, "Hey, none taken. It's was my off day. It's going to take a while to get my game back." JEFF tells them, "Well guys, both of your games haven't been back since Spring Training. We have hundred more games if we want to take this team to the pennant." RILEY tells his father, "Relax, Pop. We can fix this. We just lost one game, we'll have another chance to win." ASHLEY tells Matt, "Well, I hope so. The way you guys play. You guys need a miracle." MATT tells Ashley, "Trust me, the miracle just started." Riley is on the mound and pitches against Anaheim Angles batter in on the home plate in the baseball field. RAY'S VOICE tells the fans, "The count 1-2 on Valentine. Riley makes the pitch." Riley throws the ball hard and Valentine gets a good grip on the ball. Valentine swings his bat and hit's the ball out of the park. RAY'S VOICE tells the fans, "Valentine hits it and this ball is out of here." Roger swings his bat and gets struck out and goes back to the dugout. AL'S VOICE tells the fans, "Punjab swing and he's out. Yankees lose to the Angels 5-0." Riley throws the ball hard to Toronto Blue Jays batter and the batter hit's the ball and it's out of the park. Riley throws the ball again, Baltimore Orioles batter hit's the ball and its out of the park. Detroit Tigers batter hit's the ball where Riley pitches and he swings his bat and hit's the ball out of the park again. Chicago White Sox batter hit's the ball again and the ball is out of the park. Tampa Bay Rays batter hit's the ball out of the park from Riley's pitch. Matt tries dive down on the field and misses the ball. Kansas City Royals batter hit's the ball and David tries to catch the ball. AL'S VOICE tells the fans, "Wilson hit's it near left field." David tries to catches the ball, but the ball hits his head and ball goes up on the floor. AL'S VOICE tells the fans, "Yoder tries to catch the pop fly. But he's gets beamed for a inside the park home run." Matt tries to run an inside the park home run near home plate and tries to slide near home but slides halfway through it with Royals catcher tagging him out with a baseball. Riley throws the ball and the Baltimore Orioles batter gets hit by a pitch. Roger swings his bat and gets struck again. Roger is up at bat again and Seattle Mariners pitcher is on the mound. RAY'S VOICE tells the fans, "Bottom of the ninth, Mariners are up by two. With a tying run on first. Carey makes the pitch." Carey throws the ball hard and Roger swings his bat and gets struck out again. RAY'S VOICE tells the fans, "Punjab swings and gets struck out. The Yanks lose to the Marines two to nothing. That makes the Yankees losing streak to eighteen." Outside of LaGuardia Airport. Jeff, Matt and Riley are sitting down in their chairs waiting for their flight. Matt and Riley are eating their two classic Single Cheese burgers, biggie fries and a extra-large diet coke from Wendy's. RILEY tells Matt, "It's a good thing, LaGuardia put a Wendy's in this airport." MATT tells Riley, "It's too bad, they don't have one in Boston." RILEY tells Matt, "Hey, I'm sure we could go to one when we get to Boston." Matt accidentally got some ketchup on his cheeseburger wrapper on his right finger. RILEY tells Matt, "Hey Matt, you got something on your right cheek right over there." MATT tells Riley, "Where!" RILEY tells Matt, "The right one." Matt touches his cheek with ketchup on his fingers and the ketchup on his cheeks. Riley and Jeff starts laughing for a minute. MATT tells Riley, "Is it gone!" RILEY tells Matt, "No, I think you still has some more on your cheek." Matt still touches his right cheek on more ketchup and Jeff and Riley continue laughing. RILEY tells Matt, "I was just kidding you man." MATT tells Riley, "Funny, cute but funny." Jeff gives Matt a napkin in his right hand that he was carrying on the gate. When they bought their food. JEFF tells Matt, "Here you go, Matt." Matt grabs the napkin from Jeff and observes it for a minute. Matt wipes the ketchup on his cheek. MATT tells Jeff, "Hey Jeff, are you something you didn't want anything from Wendy's. We could've gotten you something there." JEFF tells them, "Thanks guys, I appreciate that. I'm saving my appetite for that new steakhouse I want to eat out." MATT tells Riley, "So, what's the new steakhouse you want to eat at it in Boston?" RILEY tells Matt, "Oh, I remember. It was called Red Steaks. I read about it, I heard Curt Schilling built the place a year ago. He's having a grand opening today." MATT tells Riley, "I heard about that restaurant in New York Times, when he opening this restaurant. I heard Red Steaks is like a five star restaurant. The restaurant critics already gave it good reviews even without eating there." RILEY tells them, "I definitely, want go to the restaurant tonight." JEFF tells them, "I would love to invite you guys, to that restaurant. We have a game tomorrow against Boston. I need my players to be rested. Besides, it's a grand opening I hardly doubt any of us get a seat in that restaurant." RILEY tells Matt, "Why are you still going. We can get a great seat in that restaurant, we are celebrities. Schilling and I are pals, I sure he can give us a great seat." MATT tells Riley, "Riley, were in last place. Schilling is in Chicago in an Upper Deck memorabilia autograph session this week. So, he won't be in the restaurant today. Even if you go to that restaurant without Shilling their, half of the Red Sox players will be their, they're going to laugh at your face for being washed up. I know they're about to pick a fight with you and they're about injure your arm that will lose your entire salary remember if you fight them. You remember what you told me?" RILEY tells Matt, "If I get injured, I get nothing. That's what Luigi told me. I remember I can't go to that place. I'm lucky my arm is still in one piece after that fight I had with Lavene." MATT tells Riley, "Don't worry, man. I'm going to help you get through this." RILEY tells his Dad, "I appreciate that. So, Dad are you still going to that steakhouse." JEFF tells Riley, "Well, at least I can try get a table from that place. I'll be their early before it opens." RILEY tells Jeff, "Well, good luck." Jeff cell phone rings for a minute. JEFF tells them, "It's mine." Jeff takes out his cell phone from right pants pocket and answers his cell phone. JEFF answers it, "Hello. Hey George!"

George is sitting down in his office chair and talking to Jeff on his phone. GEORGE tells Jeff, "Listen Jeff, we have a problem?" JEFF'S VOICE tells George, "What is it, George?" GEORGE tells Jeff, "Ryan is already chewing my ass out, if we don't turn this team around. He's expecting you to turn this team around." JEFF'S VOICE tells George, "Hey, I know we lost eighteen games. We won 1 game and lost eighteen. We're about to get out of our losing streak pretty soon. It will just take time." GEORGE tells Jeff, "Time is what we don't have. You guys been playing six weeks and were in dead last. Just like spring training." Jeff is talking to George on his cell phone outside the gate of LaGuardia Airport. JEFF Sarcastically tells George, "It's going to take some time, to turn this team around and the only way we can win some games, if I ask the trainer to give steroids to are players. This league already had enough trouble with steroid scandal we had a few years ago. You can forget about that." GEORGE'S VOICE tells Jeff, "Very funny, wise ass!" JEFF Sarcastically tells George, "The only way I can turn this team around. I have to work with some players to find their strengths and weakness." GEORGE'S VOICE tells Jeff, "Well, you better figure out way to turn this team around this season. You have to remember Ryan and the front office is that close to firing me and especially you. If we don't change things. So, none of us are going to have jobs next years and the Yanks will be shut down for good, if we don't do something." JEFF tells George, "What are you talking about?" GEORGE'S VOICE tells Jeff, "There is a reason, why Ryan picked you guys to play here. He's giving you guys a shot to play in this team. You guys have potential to take this team to the pennant. He's putting this club on the line for you guys." JEFF tells George, "What do you mean, he's putting this club on the line?" GEORGE'S VOICE tells Jeff, "I'll explain later. Not right now, if I were you. You better figure out a way to turn this team around this season or all us will be fired in the end of the season. That's all I can tell you, bye Jeff. JEFF tells George, "Bye George!" Jeff hangs up his phone. The airplane landed on the runway of Logan International Airport and heads to the gate. The door opens and the bellman shows Riley and Matt their hotel suite in the Lenox Hotel. The bellman is carrying their luggage. MATT tells Riley, "Man, this room is awesome. Man, Ryan knows how to treat a player." RILEY tells Matt, "I used to living like this before. It was so awesome back then." The bellman puts their luggage down on the floor. BELLMAN tells them, "Here it is, boys. Superior King Room." Riley goes over to the bellman, takes out his wallet out of his right pants pocket and takes out a hundred out of his wallet. RILEY tells the bellman, "Here you go, kid." Riley gives the hundred dollars to the bellman and bellman grabs it and observes it for a minute. BELLMAN tells Riley, "Thank you, sir. I can take the Hawaiian vacation I can dream about taking. Excuse me, Mr. Riley I wondered if I could get your autograph for a minute." RILEY tells the

Bellman, "Yeah, sure kid. Hang on a minute." Riley sees the notepad and pen on the table, grabs it and signs the autograph for the bellman. RILEY tells the Bellman, "What's your name?" BELLMAN tells Riley, "Brundon Rickford, Mr. Riley." Riley finishes signing his autograph and tears up the note and gives it to Brundon. RILEY tells Brundon, "Here you go, Brundon." Brundon grabs the note and observes it for a minute. BRUNDON tells Riley, "Thank you, sir. I appreciate that. Just let me know, if you need anything." RILEY tells Brundon, "Sure, no problemo." Brundon exit's the suite and closes the door. Matt sits down in his bed for a minute. MATT tells Riley, "Man, this room is so awesome." RILEY tells Matt, "You betcha Matt. I know Jeff, ask me for mentor program. He picked me as your roommate for the season." MATT tells Riley, "I never did ask, why do I need a roommate for the road." RILEY tells Matt, "Rookies, have to have roommates for mentoring program. Before they stay in their own room next season." MATT tells Riley, "I forgot about that rule. Let's see, if their's a movie I can order on the set today." Matt turns on the remote and see what movie he wants to watch. MATT tells Riley, "So, what hotel did you stay when you played for the minors?" RILEY tells Matt, "Mostly on the road, we stayed in Bed and Breakfast and Inns when I played for the minors." MATT tells Riley, "Pretty cool. I was going to ask you about your daughter Ashley. You guys really close." RILEY tells Matt, "Of course, were like pals. She was late bloomer growing up. When she went off to college and joined a sorority. She had the million dollar make over." MATT tells Riley, "Sounds cool. I guess she dates a lot now, since her new makeover." RILEY tells Matt, "I don't think so. She had a boyfriend who she dated for eighteen years. Lucas was a good kid and part of the family. I think they were think about getting married right after they graduate from college. They went to different schools. She was going to NYU and he was going to Yale. I don't think the commute would be tough for them, so they decided to break up before they went their separate ways. She hasn't dated anybody after Lucas." MATT tells Riley, "Man that was bad. What was she like growing up?" RILEY tells Matt, "She was a tomboy, she loved baseball like me. She was an excellent pitcher and she was the star in her softball team. All State and valedictorian of her school. She wanted to be a writer growing up. NYU has the best writing program ever." MATT tells Riley, "At least I know why she wanted to work in the library. Experience and if writing doesn't work out at least she will have a job in the library to fall back on." RILEY tells Matt, "You got that right." MATT tells Riley, "You know, it's kind of weird. But I think her roommate Jessica has a crush on you." RILEY tells Matt, "No way, you don't say." MATT tells Riley, "She does. I saw her touching your leg and I think she likes you." RILEY tells Matt, "Well, it's good for a girl like Jessica to have a crush on me. I may not look a male Abercrombie & Fitch model. I may not be a superstar athlete anymore. But, I can still land a hot girl like Jessica."

MATT tells Riley, "Well good luck, Ashley will kill you. If you're thinking about going out with her roommate." RILEY tells Matt, "Even if Jessica and me gone out. What wouldn't Ashley be okay with it?" MATT tells Riley, "She's her roommate and you're going out with a girl who was about her age. If you marry her. Ashley might call her Mom pretty soon. If you guys do break up, she might have to move out of her dorm. That's one of the main reasons, we didn't any guy shouldn't be dating somebody else sister or ex. This would happened." RILEY tells Matt, "Relax, I won't be dating her. It's too bad Jessica will have to drool around me. I am the master of landing hot women." MATT tells Riley, "Yeah right." RILEY tells Matt, "I'm going to try out the pool today. Give me a call if you need anything." MATT tells Riley, "Yeah, sure thing. I'm ordering room service right now. You want anything, when you get back." RILEY tells Matt, "No, I'm good. I'm going to change in my trunks. We have to remember, we have to be on the bus tomorrow afternoon." MATT tells Riley, "I'll remember that." Riley sees his suitcase grabs it and goes to the bathroom. MATT tells Riley, "Hey, just remember. Always stay out of the deep end." RILEY tells Matt, "Funny, cute but funny." Riley and Matt start laughing for a minute. Riley exit's his suite and closes the door in the hallway. Riley is carrying a towel and wearing swim trunks and a t-shirt. Riley heads to the elevator and wait for to open. Inside Lennox Hotel Indoor Swimming Pool. Riley enters the pool when he opens the door and sees Jessica wearing a tight red bikini in the hot tub. Riley goes over to the hot tub and puts the towel and takes off his t-shirt and puts it on the chair. Riley goes inside the hot tub and kisses Jessica. RILEY tells Jessica, "Hey kiddo." JESSICA tells Riley, "Hey honey." RILEY tells Jessica, "It's good thing I paid the pool attendant to let me have this pool all night." JESSICA tells Riley, "If we want to go somewhere else to make out. Won't your roommate Matt be there." RILEY tells Jessica, "We won't have to. We can go to your room that I paid for that's next to mine." JESSICA tells Riley, "Well, you read my mind." Jessica makes out with Riley. Matt is in Riley and Matt's Suite in Lenox Hotel. Matt is eating a cheeseburger and French fries and drinking a 20 oz bottle of diet pepsi. Matt is watching an action movie in a paid tv screen and wearing his pajamas. MATT tells himself, "I wondered if I can watch playboy in this channel." Matt's movie is over and Matt turns on the remote to the playboy tv and watch a porno. MATT tells himself, "It's a good thing, the team is paying for our expenses. I think I see a tit. Man, it's awesome. I think I died and gone to heaven." The door knocks for a minute. MATT tells himself, "I guess Riley, locked himself out of the room again. But, he'll be pleased when he sees this footage in the playboy tv." Matt pauses Playboy tv and gets up from his bed. Matt goes over to the door and opens it. MATT tells himself, "Riley, you lose your key." Matt opens the door and sees Ashley wearing tight jeans and zipped up leather jacket. MATT tells Ashley, "Ashley, what are you doing here? I didn't know you were coming?" ASHLEY tells Matt, "My dad invited me and Jessica come watch him play tomorrow. He bought a room for me and Jessica next to his. Jessica wanted to see my father action. I talked to my dad and he said yes and here we are." MATT tells Ashley, "Well come on in." ASHLEY tells Matt, "Thanks Matt." Ashley comes into the door and Matt closes it. MATT tells Ashley, "You're father is not here right now. If you want to wait for him, he'll be back in a hour." ASHLEY tells Matt, "Okay." Matt and Ashley sits down in another bed since his food in on the other bed. Ashley sees Matt watching playboy tv and it's on pause. ASHLEY tells Matt, "I hope I didn't interrupt anything important." MATT tells Ashley, "No, I was watching a movie." ASHLEY tells Matt, "What are you watching?" MATT tells Ashley, "There was a commercial on, I saw on documentary in PBS for a minute. I was about to change it." Ashley recognizes the channel for a minute. ASHLEY tells Matt, "Are you sure, it isn't Playboy TV. Because I recognize one of the girls on the channel." MATT tells Ashley, "Oh, of course not. Hang on a second." Matt gets up from the bed, grabs the remote and tries to turn it off and accidentally turns it on. MATT tells Ashley, "Oh god. I think this might be the wrong channel." Matt tries to change the channel but comes a no go. Ashley is watching hot woman masturbating on the playboy channel. Ashley recognizes one of the girls on the channel. ASHLEY tells Matt, "Hey, isn't that Kimberly Watson." MATT tells Ashley, "I think so, you know her." ASHLEY tells Matt, "She was in my history class in college and she was playmate of the month last year." MATT tells Ashley, "Gee, I didn't know that. I wondered how she gotten into this documentary." Matt tries to change the channel and falls down on the floor when he didn't see the pillow on the floor and breaks the remote. Ashley gets up from the bed and turns off the tv set with a on button and picks up Matt. Ashley giggles a little. ASHLEY tells Matt, "Remember next time you want turn on or turn off the tv always turn on the power button." MATT tells Ashley, "I remember that, I always used to turn the sets on by remote." ASHLEY tells Matt, "That was a playboy tv. You have nothing be shamed about it. I'm may not be a guy, I'm a chick I masturbate too." MATT tells Ashley, "Gee, I didn't know that. How did you know how it was Playboy tv." ASHLEY tells Matt, "Hugh Hefner was fan of my father, he invited me and my father to the playboy mansion for the summer." MATT tells Ashley, "Sounds amazing. You're not mad, I was watching playboy. Mostly any girl I know would be offensive for guys watching playboy." ASHLEY tells Matt, "Of course not. You guys are just like us. We have to masturbate once in a while. Too keep our sexual urges going. I can tell you're a virgin." Matt is a little embarrassed. MATT tells Ashley, "I am not a virgin."

ASHLEY tells Matt, "Well, I can tell you're desperate virgin. Nerdy guys who think about sex and never done it." MATT tells Ashley, "Are you a psychology major?" ASHLEY tells Matt, "No, I'm an English major. I watch a teen sex comedies and especially American Pie. You can learn a lot when you watch the movie." MATT tells Ashley, "It was my favorite movie back then." ASHLEY tells Matt, "Just want you to know, nothing to be ashamed about watching playboy tv. I do it all the time too." MATT tells Ashley, "Wow, you watch playboy tv." ASHLEY tells Matt, "No, I watch gay porno. It turned me on a bit." MATT tells Ashley, "You masturbate watching gay porno." ASHLEY tells Matt, "That, and watching a Justin Long movie always keep me masturbating." MATT tells Ashley, "You are one weird chick. I'll call the front desk and see if they can get me a new remote. I think this one broken." ASHLEY tells Matt, "You can do that or we could do this." Ashley kisses Matt for a minute and stops. MATT tells Ashley, "You do realize, I'm your father's best friend. He probably be back in this room for a minute. I don't think we should cross any boundaries." ASHLEY tells Matt, "Matt, I didn't come here to see my father. I came to see you. I took a big risk coming here and see you." MATT tells Ashley, "Ashley, I'm not exactly the kind of guy girls like you usually date. I know you usually got out of a huge relationship with Lucas. I'm not exactly a guy you should rebound with." ASHLEY tells Matt, "I'm not. I was in love with you the first time I saw Matt. You're a nice guy, I would definitely would want to be with. Tell me did you ever had a girlfriend before." MATT tells Ashley, "No one. I never dated before. I had a busy schedule, going to school playing baseball. Never had any time to date and I wasn't exactly a catch back then. I usually the guy that girls usually reject." Ashley grabs his hand and puts him down on the other bed. Matt sees her for a minute and smiles a little. ASHLEY tells Matt, "Do me a favor, Schultz Ask me out!" MATT tells Ashley, "Okay. Ashley!" Ashley takes off her tight leather jacket slowly and puts it down on the floor. Ashley is wearing a tight gray tank top and holding Matt's hand. Matt is trying to say the words for a minute and got it. MATT tells Ashley, "Ashley Riley, would you like to go out with me next week. If it's okay with you." ASHLEY tells Matt, "I got one thing say to you, Matthew!" MATT tells Ashley, "What's that?" Ashley makes out Matt for a minute and stops. ASHLEY tells Matt, "You make the reservations and I'll bring the champagne." MATT tells Ashley, "I got some better than champagne." Matt let's goes of Ashley's hand. Matt goes to fridge, opens it and takes out two bud light bottles. Matt gives Ashley her bud light beer bottle and she opens it and so does Matt. Ashley starts drinking her beer and she makes out with Matt and they stop. ASHLEY tells Matt, "Another shot!" Matt and Ashley starts drinking their beer and stop. MATT tells Ashley, "And kiss!" Matt and Ashley starts making out for a minute and stops. MATT tells Ashley, "Another shot!" Matt and Ashley starts drinking their beer and stops. ASHLEY tells Matt, "And kiss!" Matt and Ashley starts making out for a minute and drops their beer bottles down on the floor and continue making out. Matt and Ashley make out in the bed. The sun goes up and the alarm is on. Matt and Ashley are in the bed naked and Ashley is cuddling with Matt. Matt wakes up for a minute and turns off the alarm. Matt sees that Riley is not in his bed. MATT tells Ashley, "Riley, I guess he over slept in the pool. I better go get him." Matt gets up from the bed, sees his boxer shorts and puts it on. Matt wakes up Ashley for a minute. Ashley gets up for a minute. ASHLEY tells Matt, "What is it!" Ashley gets a little groggy and sees Matt for a minute and she starts smiling at him. ASHLEY tells Matt, "Hey honey!" MATT tells Ashley, "Hey baby!" Matt and Ashley starts making out for a minute and stops. MATT tells Ashley, "We have to get up and me and Riley have to be in the bus in a hour for the game. He probably overslept in the pool. I'm going to go look for him after I clean up." ASHLEY tells Matt, "You want some company." MATT tells Ashley, "I got this one." Matt and Ashley exit's the room and Matt tries to find Riley in Lenox Hotel Hallway. MATT tells Ashley, "I have to go look for Riley and tell him we have to be on the bus in a hour." ASHLEY tells Matt, "I help you find him." MATT tells Ashley, "Even if we look for him, won't he get suspicious that were looking for him together. He might get some ideas that were hooking up." ASHLEY tells Matt, "We are hooking up." MATT tells Ashley, "Yeah, he doesn't know that. When he does find out." ASHLEY tells Matt, "What would've be the worse situation if he finds out?" MATT tells Ashley, "I don't know death by strangulation or he could smash my head with a baseball bat. You do the math." ASHLEY tells Matt, "That bad, huh." MATT tells Ashley, "Riley is my best friend and my teammate. If he finds out, I'm hooking up with you. I think I'm going to end up in the Trauma Unit in Boston General." ASHLEY tells Matt, "He won't kill you, if we team up together and tell him we love each other. He'll be cool with it." MATT tells Ashley, "Good luck." ASHLEY tells Matt, "Jessica is probably worried about me. So, I'm going to check in my room for a minute and tell her I'm all right." MATT tells Ashley, "Okay, go for it!" Ashley and Matt head to her room, Ashley knocks on her door and the door opens and it's Riley and Jessica. Jessica is in her bathrobe and Riley is wearing his boxer shorts. MATT tells himself, "Oh boy, this is get interesting." ASHLEY tells them, "Dad, Jessica." RILEY tells Matt, "Hi, honey. May I ask what are you doing here with my pal Matt." MATT tells Jessica, "It's a long story, I think if we all go inside. I think we can explain ourselves." JESSICA tells Ashley, "You know Ashley, you didn't tell me your father was hot." ASHLEY tells Jessica, "Okay, I think I'm scarred for that. For eternity." JESSICA tells them, "Let's go inside and will all talk." Matt and Ashley goes inside the room and Jessica kisses Riley in the lips. RILEY tells Jessica, "You do realize, my daughter standing right next to us." JESSICA tells Riley, "I know, but that was for me for me saying hello." RILEY sarcastically tells Jessica, "What are you say will you marry me." JESSICA tells Riley, "This!" Jessica makes out with Riley and stops. RILEY tells them, "That will do it!" Jessica and Riley enters the room and Jessica closes the door where everybody explain themselves. The Yankees Bus drives to Fenway Park. Jeff is sitting in his seat right next to Matt and Riley who are having an awkward situation in the Yankees Bus. JEFF tells them, "You guys okay, looks like you guys had a long night." RILEY tells his father, "Don't ask!" MATT tells Jeff, "And don't tell." JEFF tells them, "Wasn't going to." Riley looks at Matt for a minute. RILEY tells Matt, "You saw my daughter naked?" MATT tells Riley, "Didn't you see her college roommate naked too?" RILEY tells Matt, "Yeah, let's forget about that. Ever." MATT tells Riley, "I'm with you on that one." Riley is on the pitcher's mound in the baseball field in Fenway Park and Red Sox batter is on home plate and waiting for Riley to Pitch. RAY'S VOICE tells the fans, "Bottom of the eighth and Ludge is up to bat. Riley makes the pitch." Riley throws the ball hard and Ludge hit's the ball near second and third base. Matt is that close to catch the ball. AL'S VOICE tells the fans, "Ludge makes the hit and hits it near second and third and Schultz tries to make the catch." Matt is that close to catch the ball and the ball beams on to Matt's head and the ball goes up to near head. RAY'S VOICE tells the fans, "Gets beamed on the head and the runner on third steals home." Matt head hurts for a minute, grabs the ball from the grass and throws the ball at home plate. RAY'S VOICE tells the fans, "Rodriguez makes it to home plate. Schultz grabs the ball and throws it to home." The ball goes up to home and the Yankees Catcher catches the ball but the ball hit's the catcher's mask and the catcher falls down on the floor and Rodriguez scores the winning run. RAY'S VOICE tells the fans, "Lupz tries to catch the ball, but he gets beamed on the head and falls down. Where Rodrigurez makes the score and he's safe." HOME PLATE UMPIRE tells the batter, "Safe!" AL'S VOICE tells the fans, "The Red Sox lead four to nothing." Ryan, George and Reynolds are sitting down in their chairs watching the game in their luxury box. REYNOLDS tells them, "Looks like this team is in the bag for me." RYAN tells Reynolds, "You never know, Reynolds. This team will turn around." REYNOLDS tells George, "Yeah, when. Until I'm qualified for social security." GEORGE tells Reynolds, "It's bottom of the eighth. They'll turn this team around." Riley is on the mound and looks at batter in home plate two players on second and third in the baseball field. RAY'S VOICE tells the fans, "Were still bottom of the eighth and were two down. Riley is 3 to 2 on Salty. Riley makes the pitch." Riley throws the ball hard and Salty swings his bat and strikes out. AL'S VOICE tells the fans, "Salty swings and he's out. Riley retires the side and the Red Sox lead 5 to nothing to the Yankees." The Yankees Pitching

Coach sees how much target speed did Riley pitched in his radar gun in the Dug Out Box. Jeff goes over to the Yankees Pitching Coach and talks to him. JEFF tells Yankees Pitching Coach, "How much this time?" YANKEES PITCHING COACH tells Jeff, "102!" JEFF tells the Yankees Pitching Coach, "Michael has still have some good pitching heat. But he still doesn't know how to control it." YANKEES PITCHING COACH tells Jeff, "We still need to help him get his game back. His pitching arm is back, but we still need to adjust it right." JEFF tells the Yankees Pitching Coach, "That's something I have to work on." Two Yankees batters are on first and second base and Matt is up to bat in the baseball field. Ashley and Jessica are sitting next to the dugout box near his father is at and Ashley sees Matt ready to bat. JESSICA tells Ashley, "I guess you're boyfriend is up?" ASHLEY tells Jessica, "He's not my boyfriend." JESSICA tells Ashley, "What were you doing in his hotel room? Playing Parcheesi with the same clothes you were wearing last night." ASHLEY tells Jessica, "And you having sex with my father is what trying to get back at me. For what for using your tooth brush. You were supposed to be my best friend, dating my father is crossing the line." JESSICA tells Ashley, "I'm not crossing any lines all right. I'm not getting back at you for anything. I really like your dad. What about you sleeping with your teammate's father is crossing the line with him. What will he think of you?" ASHLEY tells Jessica, "The truth is, I really do like him. He's a good guy, I'm not doing this to get back at my dad. I want to be with him." JESSICA tells Ashley, "I think you should tell Matt sometimes." ASHLEY tells Jessica, "I should. But I don't want you to hurt my father. My mom died two years ago. He hasn't dated anybody after she died. I just don't want you to hurt him for anything." JESSICA tells Ashley, "I would never do that. Besides, he was thinking asking me to marry him. But he ask me to ask your permission first. If it's okay with you, I want to marry him in the end of the season." ASHLEY tells Jessica, "Look Jess, whether I say yes or no. This is up to my father and I wanted to ask you, do you love him." JESSICA tells Ashley, "Yes, I do." ASHLEY tells Jessica, "You have my blessing and please don't talk about your sex life with my dad right in front of me. I'm about to hurl right now." Jessica is really happy right now. JESSICA tells Ashley, "I appreciate that, I was going to tell you what I call sex with Riley is called Romp Bust...?" Ashley interrupts Jessica for a minute. ASHLEY tells them, "Hey, hey not in front of the kids." Matt is on home plate and waiting for the pitch from the Red Sox Pitcher. AL'S VOICE tells the fans, "Top of the ninth, two runners are in first and second. The Red Sox lead five to three. Schultz is the go ahead run on plate. O'Reilly waits for a signal." Red Sox gives him a signal and it's the right one for O'Reilly. RAY'S VOICE tells the fans, "O'Reily got what he's looking for. O'Reilly makes the pitch." O'Reilly throws the ball hard and Matt swings his bat and hits it hard. The ball goes up to pop fly. AL'S VOICE tells the fans, "Schultz swings and hit's a pop fly. And he's out." The Red Sox catcher catches the ball and the ball games over. RAY'S VOICE tells the fans, "That retires the side and the ball games over. Red Sox wins this five-three." AL'S VOICE tells the fans, "And this makes the Yankees Losing streak to twelve right now." RAY'S VOICE tells the fans, "It's going to take a miracle for this team to turn around. Just hope Jeff Linwood will figure out what to do before this season is over or adios job for Jeff Linwood and the rest of the team." Matt feels bad about what happened and heads back to the dugout box. Ryan, George and Reynolds are sitting down in their chairs and Reynolds is applauding for Yankees losing again and laughing too in the Luxury Box in Fenway Park. REYNOLDS tells Ryan, "Thank you, guys for entertaining me today. I haven't had a good laugh in weeks, when Ryan let's his pants down when he forgot to button his pants." RYAN tells Reynolds, "Actually that was you, pulling my pants down." REYNOLDS tells them, "I know, but it was funny. To me. I guess the Yankees are right 8 to twenty right now and reaching dead last. I guess this team is going to be mine right now. Why don't you boys sign the contract to this team to me right now?" GEORGE tells Reynolds, "Season's not over yet, Reynolds." REYNOLDS tells George, "It is too me." GEORGE tells Reynolds, "Don't worry, this team will turn around in a minute. You'll see." REYNOLDS tells George, "Don't make me laugh George. I actually you just did." Reynolds laughs again really loud and stops. REYNOLDS tells them, "I hope you losers you losers hand me the contract to your team when the season is over. When I sign it, seal it and demolish it. Keep up the good work boys." Reynolds gets up from his chairs and continues laughing. Reynolds exit's the luxury box right now. RYAN tells George, "I like you pound the shit out of him right now." GEORGE tells Ryan, "You do that, you'll make it worse." RYAN tells George, "We better turn this team around pretty soon or were going to have sign over the team to Reynolds." GEORGE tells Ryan, "I better go call Riley tell him what's going on." RYAN tells George, "You better tell him, our asses our on the line here. Not just ours, but the team is. If we don't turn this team around, all of us will have to kiss our jobs good-bye." GEORGE tells Ryan, "You got it Ryan. I better go talk to them." George gets up from his chair and heads to the phone. Matt is getting dressed and is about to put his shirt on in the Yankees Locker Room. Until Ashley enters the locker room and sees Matt for a minute. Ashley is a little speechless seeing Matt shirtless. ASHLEY tells Matt, "Oh, I'm sorry." MATT tells Ashley, "Me too! I didn't know you were coming here." ASHLEY tells Matt, "Me neither. I was just looking for my dad." MATT tells Ashley, "Well, he's not here. Hang on a second." Matt puts his shirt on for a minute and he did. ASHLEY tells Matt, "You know where he is?" MATT tells Ashley, "He's in the shower?" ASHLEY tells Matt, "Well, I'll wait.

Tough game. I'm sorry you guys lost." MATT tells Ashley, "Well, we just made our losing streak to thirteen right now." ASHLEY tells Matt, "Well, don't worry you guys will figure out. One thing I learned about sports, their always way out. With hard work and determination, their always way out." MATT tells Ashley, "Right now, this team needs a miracle to survive." ASHLEY tells Matt, "It does, you and my dad are the miracle. I think it was fate they brought you guys here to turn this team around." MATT tells Ashley, "I think our fate is wrong. I think they got the wrong guys to pick to turn this team this around." ASHLEY tells Matt, "One thing, I always learned from my father. Never back down, you stick with it and work hard. I think fate will give you what you're looking for." MATT tells Ashley, "Riley actually said that." ASHLEY tells Matt, "I saw that on an episode in the Gilmore Girls. It was on cable yesterday." MATT tells Ashley, "Right now, I think I could face Riley now. I think it will be awkward with him. Since you and I are going out." ASHLEY tells Matt, "Well, it's not awkward with him dating my roommate. But at least I let it go. Give them my blessings. I just hope he could give me our blessings." MATT tells Ashley, "Ashley, I'm his best friend and his teammate. Dating you, is like crossing the line when you dating your best friend's sister or cousin or their ex. I think right now, he would kick my ass for doing that." ASHLEY tells Matt, "Look, I'll talk to him about it. Who I date, is not his business." Riley sees Matt and Ashley and it's total awkward seeing your best friend dating his daughter and Riley body is covered with a towel. Riley looks upset at Matt right now and decide not to get mad. Riley goes over talk to Ashley and Matt. RILEY tells Ashley, "Hey honey, what are you doing here?" ASHLEY tells Riley, "I came to see you, to see how are you doing?" RILEY tells Ashley, "I'm good, just hope we can pass this awkward moment between us and put it behind us." ASHLEY tells Matt, "I'm sure we can." MATT tells Ashley, "Let's just put it behind us." ASHLEY tells Matt, "I have go back to the hotel room. Me and Jessica has flight out tomorrow. Bye Pop." MATT tells Ashley, "Bye honey." Ashley kisses Matt on the cheek and leaves. Riley sees her daughter leaving and he's very upset at Matt for a minute. RILEY tells Matt, "I can't believe you're going out with my daughter." MATT tells Riley, "You're going out with your daughter's roommate how weird is that?" RILEY tells Matt, "Hey, I really like Jessica." MATT tells Riley, "I also like Ashley too, if you don't want me to date her anymore. I'll step aside." RILEY tells Matt, "Tell you the truth, I want you to step aside. But I don't, I can see why Ashley likes you, she was a late bloomer. I can see how beautiful and kind she became, just like her mother. She always picked well, liked her." MATT tells Riley, "I know she's been out of a huge relationship. But I really care about her and I would never cross that line with you or her if I break with her or cheat on her." RILEY tells Matt, "Good, if you think about it. I will kick your ass." MATT tells Riley,

"Okay, then." Riley punches Matt in the face lightly and stops. RILEY tells Matt, "Just in case, if you think about it. I will do it again, if you ever think about crossing that line." MATT tells Riley, "I won't." Jeff exits his office and talks to Matt and Riley. JEFF tells them, "Schultz, Riley. I need to see you guys right now." MATT tells Jeff, "This doesn't look good." RILEY tells Matt, "No, it doesn't." Riley and Schultz enters Jeff's office. Jeff is sitting down in his chair in his office and Riley and Matt enters the office. Matt closes the door and wait for Jeff to talk. RILEY ask his father, "You wanted to see us, Skip!" Riley sees Jeff's face and it doesn't look good. RILEY tells Matt, "This doesn't look good." JEFF tells them, "Listen guys, sit down. There's something I want to talk you about?" MATT tells Jeff, "If it's okay with you, Jeff. Will stand." JEFF tells them, "Whatever you want. I had got a call from George Jackson." RILEY tells them, "Our team's GM." JEFF tells them, "That's him and he's really disappointed about how you guys are performing. We've been in a losing streak for the last six weeks. We just extended our losing streak to twelve. I'm trying to figure out why were in a losing streak. Too bad their's only twenty-five players. Too bad I can't trade them, send them to the minors or kick them out. The only I can do is find the dead wood. That's causing our losing streak" Riley and Matt is a little nervous for a minute. MATT tells Jeff, "Did you figure out who the dead wood is, Skip!" JEFF tells them, "If I can find it, I can get rid of them and maybe can get out of our slump. But I think I figure out who it is. It all starts four of them." RILEY tells Jeff, "Who are the four that are deadwood." Matt is a little more nervous than Riley. MATT is whispering to Riley, "Please don't let that be us!" JEFF tells them, "Here are the four, David Yoder, Roger Punjab and you two." RILEY tells Jeff, "I knew it." JEFF tells Riley, "Yoder and Punjab are not the problems. I can work with them, but you two are guys are the ones giving this team a bad name. I trying to figure out how to work with you guys. What do you think I should do with you two? "RILEY tells Jeff, "We don't know, what you think?" JEFF tells Riley, "Riley, you have a great pitching arm. But your temper and your control is not working as I thought. You've been fighting with opposing players and umpires for the last few weeks. The league already fined you over eight thousand dollars. I don't want this league to fine you again. I'm trying to figure out how to get your pitching arm back, I haven't figure out yet. What do you think happened to it?" RILEY Sarcastically tells his father, "Maybe I Iced too many times or put mustard. That made me go into my slump." JEFF tells them, "Funny, Michael. Schultz, you have great speed and great hitting power for the inside the park home run. But your speed is going halfway. I'm trying to figure out what is wrong with your speed power, you can barely make it home before being tagged out. I'm trying to figure out why you're going half way. You're supposed to go full speed." MATT sarcastically tells Jeff, "I don't know, maybe I'm scared to blew my knee out or my running power doesn't work like it used too." JEFF tells them, "One thing I know about Punjab, he has great hitting power. But he can't hit the fastball and Yoder has trouble trying to catch the ball. At least I can find their strengths and weakness to work on. But finding your guys strengths and weakness is hard to find. I have three options, number one I am considering sending you back to the minors." RILEY tells Jeff, "Number two!" JEFF tells them, "I can trade you guys." MATT tells Jeff, "What's the final option?" JEFF tells Matt, "I can release you two guys." MATT tells Jeff, "What have you decided on?" JEFF tells them, "I'm sending both of you guys back to the minors. You know why?" RILEY tells Jeff, "I'm afraid to guess." JEFF tells them, "If I trade you, there won't be any team in the majors will take you. Second, if I released you it wouldn't solve anything. Plus, you might sue the club. I don't think the club could afford that right now, since were in the middle of the season." MATT tells Jeff, "So, you're going to dump us back to the minors." JEFF tells Matt, "It's the only option I can think of and I think it's whats best for the club. Since, you guys are performing well. If you guys go back and get your game back. I call you guys back up." RILEY tells his father, "Aah man, come on Dad. You can't send us back to the minors. I'm begging you." Riley is frightened about this and Jeff is trying to figure out what to do. RILEY tells Jeff, "Come on, Jeff I have a daughter to support and my career is on the line. If I get sent back to the minors, I could lose my endorsement deals and my home. Those endorsement deals their bread and butter. I can't support my family without it. I can't believe you would do that to your own son and granddaughter. Besides, I'll be out of this sport in two years what is my daughter is going to live on, if I get sent back or don't get that ten mil for two years." JEFF tells Riley, "I heard about it. Your agent, trying to persuade me to up your salary to ten mil. But your game isn't performing and the club won't up your salary if you don't approve Mike." RILEY tells his Dad, "Did they also tell you, if I get injured for this season. I get nothing." JEFF tells them, "Yeah, they told me. Guys, I like you. You guys aren't doing so good and your game hasn't come around as I thought. I thought sending you back to the minors for the best thing for you guys." MATT tells Jeff, "Look Jeff, I don't have nothing. This is my second chance to get back in the game. I almost lost my shot, I'm not going to lose it again. All we want is a second chance." JEFF tells Matt, "I don't know guys, if I don't send you guys back to the minors. They club could fire me and they'll send you back to the minors themselves." MATT tells Jeff, "Come on Jeff, give us another chance. Will improve and will try better. Whenever there is practice. Well practice better." RILEY tells Jeff, "I'll improve my pitching game or whatever. Whatever you want, I'll do it. Anything, please I want to be on this team." JEFF tells them, "Hang on a second!" Jeff grabs the phone and starts dialing for a minute. JEFF calls George, "Hello Mr. Jackson. Listen, I need a favor. I wondered if you let my two worse players stay a little longer in this organization. Please, just give them a chance to. They'll improve and they'll do whatever I say from now on. I'll make it better for them and this team. You'll never give them chance to improve if you don't let them. I'm willing to give them a chance, how about you and this team. Trust me, they can turn this team around, if you let them. Okay, okay. I'm responsible for them. And it's my job on the line. I know, it's my ass on the line. Okay, bye." Jeff hangs up his phone and talks to Riley and Matt. JEFF tells them, "Well, guys I talk to the GM. He's willing letting you stay on this team." RILEY tells Jeff, "All right, that's great." JEFF tells them, "You guys are on probation for a month. If you guys don't win a few game and your game doesn't improve. You guys will be sent back to the minors. His words, not mine." MATT tells Jeff, "Look Jeff, give us another chance and will improve." RILEY tells Jeff, "How are we going to get our games back and Dad we need your help." JEFF tells Riley, "I don't know, if I could help you guys. I willing to help you, but how do I know you won't mess it up and it don't cost me my job." RILEY tells Jeff, "Please will do anything and remember. You're responsible for us, is not just our ass on the line here. It's yours too." JEFF tells them, "Begged a little bit harder." Matt and Riley gets up from their chairs and gets on their knees and starts begging for a minute. RILEY tells his father,

"Please sir, I need your help! " MATT tells Jeff, "You're the greatest manager in this team. You took a chance on us. We need your help, we have nowhere else to go. We have nothing left, please!" Riley and Matt cry a little. JEFF tells Riley, "Both of you guys get up!" Matt and Riley gets up from the floor and talks to Jeff. JEFF tells Riley, "All right, I'll help you guys out. But you mess up anyway. I'll revoke your probation a little earlier than a month. Both of you guys will be out of the major leagues for good. Okay!" RILEY tells Jeff, "Yes, yes Anything!" JEFF tells Riley, "The only way I can turn this team around is work on you two guys and Punjab and Yoder! I have an idea, tell Punjab and Yoder too meet me in the lobby tomorrow morning at nine. I have someplace to take you." RILEY tells Jeff, "Where are you taking us?" JEFF tells them, "I'll show you when we get there. Go tell them to meet me us in the lobby tomorrow morning at nine." RILEY tells Jeff, "Okay, you got it Pop. Thanks for giving us a second chance we owe you." JEFF tells them, "Hey, no problemo. Just here to help." Mike and Riley heads to the door, Riley opens the door. Mike and Riley exit's Jeff's office and Riley closes the door. Riley and Matt exit's the office and talk to each other in the Yankees Locker Room. RILEY tells Matt, "Look Matt, let's put our difference aside who were dating and let's concentrate on ourselves and this team. They're depending on us." MATT tells Riley, "You got it!" Matt shakes Riley's hand and let's go. MATT tells Riley, "It is weird for you dating Jessica?"

RILEY tells Matt, "It's not weird and I'm good looking and look whose talking. Dating my daughter is totally weird." MATT tells Riley, "It is not weird. You're weird." RILEY tells Matt, "No, you're weird." MATT tells Riley, "You're weird and gross!" RILEY tells Matt, "Your Mom is weird and gross." MATT tells Riley, "Is not!" RILEY tells Matt, "Is too!" Riley and Matt finds Punjab and Yoder. Jeff is on the phone with George in his office at Fenway Park. JEFF calls George on the phone, "I told you it worked. Mission Accomplish old buddy." Outside the Lenox Hotel Lobby. Matt, Riley, Jeff, David and Roger exiting the lobby and stops for a minute. Jeff is waiting for his valet to get his car. DAVID tells Matt, "So, Jeff where is this place you're taking us?" MATT tells Jeff, "And this place could help us improve our games." JEFF tells Riley, "You betcha, don't worry you'll see it when we get there. Since, this is our off day." RILEY tells himself, "I was afraid of that." Jeff's 2010 Ford Tarus outside the lobby and parks right in front of the sidewalk. The door opens and it's the Valet. The Valet closes the door and carries the valet ticket and goes over talk to Jeff. The Valet gives Jeff his ticket. THE VALET tells Jeff, "Here you go, sir!" JEFF tells the Valet, "Thank you." Jeff takes out his wallet from his right pants pocket, takes out twenty dollars and gives it to the Valet. JEFF tells the Valet, "Here you go?" The valet grabs the twenty dollars and observes it for a minute. THE VALET tells Jeff, "Thank you sir." JEFF tells the Valet, "Hey, no problemo." Jeff puts his wallet back in right pants pocket. JEFF tells them, "Come on, guys. Let's go!" MATT tells them, "I hate to see where he's taking us?" RILEY tells Matt, "Whatever it is, I don't think it's not Six Flags." Matt, Riley, Jeff, David and Roger gets in Jeff's car. Jeff starts the car and exits the hotel. Jeff, Matt, Riley, David and Roger enters the little league baseball field in Princeton New Jersey. Matt, Riley, David and Roger sees the baseball equipment on the baseball field for a minute near home plate. DAVID tells Jeff, "So, what is that place?" JEFF tells them, "This is the baseball field where I coached my company's little league baseball team and where I took them to a championship. If I could get through 9-12 years old and make them great players and get them to a championship. I can get you guys and the Yanks to the pennant." MATT tells Jeff, "How are you going to do that?" JEFF tells Matt, "By looking at strength and weakness and see what I can work with. I already checked them out in the game tapes, what were doing wrong. I think I can help you guys look for you strength and weakness to help you guys improve." MATT tells Jeff, "How exactly are you going to help us improve, skipper?" JEFF tells Riley, "I'll show you. Riley, Yoder grab a mit and a ball." RILEY tells Jeff, "Okay. Riley and David heads to home plate and grabs some baseball gloves and Riley grabs a baseball from the equipment bag and goes back to Jeff, Matt, Riley, David and Roger talk to them. DAVID tells Jeff, "We got the gloves and the ball. Now what?" JEFF tells David, "Yoder, I need you to be the catcher. Riley were going to work on your pitching. I already saw the game tapes, you have the heat. But you can't pitch straight near the glove. We have to work on that. I have on an idea about that." Jeff takes out peanut butter M&M's and gives it to Riley. Riley grabs the peanut butter M&M's and observes it for a minute. JEFF tells Riley, "You're not allergic to peanuts are you?" RILEY tells his father, "No." JEFF tells Riley, "Good, eat one." David is in catcher's position and waiting for the pitch. Riley eats a peanut butter M&M and throws the pitch hard. The ball hits David glove hard and David throws the ball back to Riley. Jeff sees the target speed on the radar gun for a minute. RILEY tells Jeff, "How much!" JEFF tells Riley, "84!" RILEY tells Jeff, "What, I can't even pitch harder than that. I just can't do it!" JEFF tells Riley, "Yes, you can Mikey. But you're mind is somewhere else. I'll show you, throw it again." Riley throws the ball hard, the ball misses the glove and hit's the fence. Riley kicks the dirt on the mound and is really upset for a minute. RILEY tells Jeff, "I can't do it. I don't even know why you guys want me back. I am washed up, I couldn't save my wife. I couldn't even strke out Lavene. It just shows he's a bigger jerk than I thought." JEFF tells Riley, "Michael, calm down." RILEY tells Jeff, "Why is it guys like Lavene stay in majors become hot shot players and guys like me get dumped in the minors and get the shaft." Jeff snaps his fingers hard. JEFF tells Riley, "Riley, blaming it on your wife's cancer or Lavene is not going to help you get your game back. You have to take responsibility for yourself first. The only way you can do that, stop blaming yourself." RILEY tells his father, "I can't Jeff, the only reason why I can't pitch so good. Because every time I think of my wife dying and Lavene mocking me. I lose my control and I forget everything else. It's one of the main reasons, why I got sent to the minors in the first place. I think you should've cut me in the first place." JEFF tells his son, "No, I was right to let you play here. I found a way to get your game back." RILEY tells Jeff, "How's that?" JEFF tells his son "What is one thing that always gives you a joy?" RILEY "When I ate this peanut butter M&M, it got me to stop thinking about Lavene and Linda dying. But if I ever could tell her up their, that I want to pitch again. She would be right by my side and tell me it's okay." JEFF tells Riley, "I have an idea, eat two of those M&M's." RILEY tells his father, "What, just trust me?" Jeff eat two peanut butter M&M's out of his pocket. JEFF tells Riley, "Close your eyes and tell my daughter-in-law and your wife Linda and say to her I want to pitch again five times." Riley closes his eyes and say to his wife for a minute. RILEY tells Jeff, "I want to pitch again, I want to pitch again, I want to pitch again, I want to pitch again, I want to pitch again!" JEFF tells Riley, "Open them." Riley opens his eyes for a minute. JEFF tells Riley, "How do you feel now, kid!" RILEY tells his father, "I'll show you!" Riley makes the pitch, throws the ball hard and the ball hits David's glove hard. Jeff sees the pitch on the radar gun.

Riley looks at Jeff for a minute. JEFF tells Riley, "101, a couple more." Riley throws the ball hard two more times and Jeff sees the radar gun and gives Riley a thumbs up. Jeff works on Matt and Matt is up on bat and waiting for Riley to pitch. JEFF tells Matt, "The reason why you can't run a triple or inside the park homerun. You're out of focus. You need a target or a bull's-eye to get you going. Focus on that fence right their make it look like a bull's-eye you want to hit. Picture the third or fourth base like a second bull's-eye, if you want to go third make it look like a bulls eye. If you want to go fourth also make it look like a bull's-eye. Just remember, always look at the target and score a bull's-eye on it. Okay." MATT tells Jeff, "I'll try it." JEFF tells Riley, "Michael, make the pitch." Jeff exit's the home plate and Matt is up to bat. Matt looks at the center field fence and picture it as a bulls eye. Riley makes the pitch, Matt hit's the ball hard and the ball hit's the centerfield fence. Matt drops the ball and looks at third base as a target where David is playing third base. Roger grabs the ball from the ground, throws it to David and Matt slides through third base and David caught the ball near third base and doesn't tag Matt out. He slided on to third on time. Jeff calls the play. JEFF tells Matt, "He was safe." Matt gets up from the floor and is relieved that he got his game back. MATT tells Jeff, "All right, I did it. I did it, I got my game back." JEFF tells Matt, "You got a long way to go kid." Roger is on home plate and ready to bat and Jeff motivates him for a minute. JEFF tells

Roger, "Just remember, when you see the ball. Picture it somebody push you around and hit it. Look it and hit it. Okay!" ROGER tells Jeff, "I'll try." JEFF tells Riley, "Michael, hit it!" Jeff exits the home plate, Riley throws the ball and Roger pictures the ball as his father. IMAGINARY ROGER'S DAD tells Roger, "You never be good enough, why don't you put away this baseball nonsense, go back to work with me and marry the woman your mother and I arrange for you!" Roger is upset for a minute. ROGER tells himself, "No!" Roger swings his bat and hit's the ball out of the park. Riley throws another pitch and sees his imaginary father laughing at him. ROGER tells himself, "No!" Roger swings his bat and hit's the ball out of the park. Jeff is working with David about his catching. Figures out how to motivate him. JEFF tells David, "Picture your favorite food you like to eat and catch it." DAVID tells Jeff, "I'll try skipper." Jeff heads to home plate, grabs the bat and ball near the plate and sees Jeff in Centerfield. JEFF tells David, "Centerfield." Jeff throws the ball in the air, swings his bat and when the ball comes down. Jeff hit's the ball near centerfield where David is at and supposed to catch. David sees the ball for a minute and wait for it to. DAVID tells Jeff, "Think, favorite food. Favorite food! What is my favorite food, oh yeah the pie that my Mom makes me. Rhubarb Pie!" David pictures the ball as a rhubarb pie and the ball goes near centerfield wall. David runs to centerfield wall, jumps up and catches the ball. Jeff hits another ball nears the center field grass, David pictures the ball as a rhubarb pie again and dives down the grass and catches it. Jeff smiling for a minute. JEFF tells himself, "We have a long way to go." Jeff hits another ball near the centerfield wall. The ball goes up in the air near the centerfield wall in the baseball field and David catches it. AL'S VOICE tells the fans, "What a spectacular catch." RAY'S VOICE tells the fans, "I don't believe it too." Red Sox pitcher throws the ball hard and Matt is up at bat. Matt pictures the left field wall as a bull's-eye and swings his bat. Matt hit's the ball near left field wall and drops his bat. Matt runs all three bases and pictures the home plate as a bull's-eye. AL'S VOICE tells the fans, "Schultz will go all the way." Red Sox outfielder grabs the ball from the grass and throws it to home plate. RAY'S VOICE tells the fans, "This might be an inside the park homerun." The ball is near the catcher and the ball hit's the glove. Matt slides through home plate and the Red Sox catcher is supposed to tag him out. Matt slides through home plate, before the catcher tags him out and the home plate umpire makes the call. RAY'S VOICE tells the fans, "Schultz slides and he's…?" Home plate umpire interrupts Ray's commentary for a minute. HOME PLATE UMPIRE tells Schulz, "Safe!" AL'S VOICE tells the fans, "Schultz scored a second run and were tied 2-2!" Red Sox pitcher throws the ball and Roger is up at bat and Roger pictures his father as the baseball. IMAGINARY ROGER'S DAD tells Roger, "You'll never be good enough!" Roger gets upset, swings his bat and hit's the ball out of the park. RAY'S VOICE tells the fans, "It's out of their. Punjab scores the winning run and gives the Yankees the lead 3-2." Riley is on the mound and Red Sox batter is on home plate ready to bat. AL'S VOICE tells the fans, "It's bottom of the ninth, the Yanks are on the lead with one run ahead. Riley makes the pitch." Riley throws the ball hard and Red Sox batter swings his bat and strikes out. RAY'S VOICE tells the fans, "And he's out. This would make eleventh strike out in the afternoon. His game has been improving and this is the final out. If Riley's get the final batter out and Yanks will win and their losing streak up to nineteen? Looks who's up to bat." The next Red Sox exit's the Red Sox dugout box and heads to home plate. AL'S VOICE tells the fans, "Linwood Morrow, he was last year's golden glove winner, 300 rbi's and hit 41 homers last season. He hit two homers off at Riley head in this game." Riley has to think and Riley knows what to do. Riley looks at the umpire for a minute. RILEY tells the guys, "Time, I need to talk to Schultz for a minute. Schultz get in here." HOME PLATE UMPIRE makes the call, "Time!" Matt goes over to the mound and talk to Riley. MATT tells Riley, "What is it Riley?" RILEY tells Matt, "Guess who's up to bat again?" MATT tells Riley, "You mean Morrow!" RILEY tells Matt, "He hit two homeruns off my head for the entire game. If I don't get him out, will lose the game again. We need to get out of this losing streak." MATT tells Riley, "We need a miracle to get him out. Are you sure, you don't want Jeff take you out of the game." RILEY tells Matt, "No, I'm going to finish this game. I need your help, what do I do?" MATT tells Riley, "Too bad you're out of your peanut butter M&m's. But I have an idea." RILEY tells Matt, "What is it?" MATT tells Riley, "Just pretend Morrow is me and listen to everything that comes out of my mouth. Trust me." RILEY tells Matt, "I beg your pardon." MATT tells Riley, "Just trust me." Matt exit's the mound and Riley sees him leaving and tells himself. RILEY tells Mike, "What the hell he's talking about." Riley is ready to pitch and sees Morrow that's up to bat. RAY'S VOICE tells the fans, "Conference is over and Riley is ready to pitch." AL'S VOICE tells the fans, "Morrow is ready to bat." Ray sees the signals on the Yankees catcher and Riley nods his head that he's ready. Ryan, George and Reynolds are sitting down in their chairs in there Luxury Box in Fenway Park. Reynolds looks at Riley for a minute. REYNOLDS tells them, "Mr. M&M is goanna choke." GEORGE tells Reynolds, "He's not goanna choke." REYNOLDS tells Ryan, "Trust me, he's going to choke. You should've let the moron stayed in the minors where he belonged. Especially that new guy Schultz." RYAN tells Reynolds, "Relax Reynolds, Riley is not going to choke." Ryan whispers to George. RYAN is Whispering to George, "Is he!" GEORGE is Whispering to Ryan, "Were about to find out pretty soon. Just hope Jeff knows what he's doing." Back in baseball field. Riley is ready to pitch, until he hears a voice coming out of nowhere. MATT'S VOICE tells the Riley, "Hey Riley, you're going to choke. Trust me, you are. No wonder you're wife kick the bucket that way she doesn't see you being washed up by yourself. Your daughter thanks of you…?" Riley sees Morrow up to bat and he's really angry. Matt's voice continues to rant. MATT'S VOICE tells Riley, "Washed up player. She's right, your daughter and your wife thinks of you as a loser. Tell you truth there that close to leaving you than this club. What do you say loser, you want to show me what washed up is?" Matt's voice laughs really hard and that makes Riley mad. RILEY tells himself, "No!" Riley throws the ball hard and Morrow sees the ball coming on real fast. Morrow swings his bat, misses and gets a strike. The ball that Riley threw comes on really hard when the ball hit's the catcher's glove. RAY'S VOICE tells the fans, "Riley makes the pitch and gets a strike." HOME PLATE UMPIRE tells the player, "Strike!" AL'S VOICE tells the fans, "You see that pitch." Jeff sees the target speed on the radar gun and it's 100. Riley throws the ball hard again and Morrow swings his bat again, misses and gets another strike. HOME PLATE UMPIRE tells the batter, "Strike 2!" Jeff sees that pitch on the radar gun and the speed is 101. Riley makes another pitch and throws the ball hard again. RAY'S VOICE tells the fan, "Riley makes another pitch and he needs one more strike to win the game." Morrow swings his bat, misses and the ball hit's the catcher's glove and it stings a little. HOME PLATE UMPIRE tells the batter, "Strike 3, you're out!" AL'S VOICE tells the fans, "The Yankees win and out of their Eighteenth losing streak ever!" RAY'S VOICE tells the fans, "The first win for Riley back at the Yanks." The players went over to congratulate him and so do the other players that came out of the dugout box. Jeff sees Riley for a minute. JEFF tells Riley, "I knew you could do it, kid! Matt and Riley are about to change in the Fenway Park locker room and all the players are congratulating them. Riley looks at Matt for a minute. RILEY tells Matt, "Thanks man, I owe you." MATT tells Riley, "You would've done the same thing for me." Jeff sees Matt and Riley goes over talk to them. JEFF tells them, "I told you guys can do it. I'm proud of you guys." MATT tells Jeff, "Thanks Jeff." Riley tells his father, "Sure thing, Pop!" JEFF tells Riley, "For a reward, I have a surprise for you guys." RILEY ask his Dad, "What is it?" Jeff takes out two baseball cards out of his left jacket pocket and gives it to Riley and Matt. Riley and Matt grabs the baseball cards from Jeff and observes it for a minute. JEFF tells them, "This!" RILEY tells Jeff, "Are very own baseball cards." JEFF tells them, "I called Upper Deck and they said your cards are ready for you. You earned it and how would you guys like to make a commercial for ballpark and Nike and make an appearance from Leno." RILEY tells Matt, "I would've said, I'm in. But, I want to wait for that until we get to the pennant." MATT tells them, "Me too, are team and our girlfriends will have to come first." JEFF tells them, "Okay, you're choice. First of all,

Matt that is my granddaughter you're talking about." Matt tells Jeff, "Sorry Jeff." Jeff laughs for a minute and tells Jeff, "I'm just kidding." Matt tells Jeff, "Funny, cute but funny." Jeff tells Matt, "Anyway, too bad, ballpark was going to five million each for the commercial. RILEY tells Jeff, "I say, let's not turn that down. But I have a suggestion that all of us are in the commercial. Not just me and Matt. "JEFF tells Riley, "You got it. That's the reason why I love you guys." Jeff hugs Matt and Riley for a minute. Matt and Riley starts laughing for a minute and stops. Ryan, George and Reynolds are sitting down in their chairs in there Luxury Box in Fenway Park. GEORGE tells Reynolds, "I told you they win Reynolds." REYNOLDS tells them, "It's just one win, they can't win it all. Trust me, those losers are going to crash and burn. One win won't change anything. Trust me, these losers are in dead last, they're going to stay in last not while I'm around." GEORGE tells Reynolds, "Will see about that." Matt walks up to the cemetery walks up to his mother's grave for a minute. Matt flashes back with a moment with her Mom. Young Matt sees the seats near the dugout box and flashes back when his Mom took him to the Yankees game when he was ten in Yankees Stadium. YOUNG MATT tells Matt's Mom, "I think that's our seats Mom." MATT'S MOM tells Young Matt, "It sure is honey." Young Matt and Matt's mom has seats near the Yankees dugout box. Young Matt sees the Yankees and Red Sox Players warming up. YOUNG MATT tells Matt's Mom,

"Someday, that will be me up their playing in the American League Championship." MATT'S MOM tells Young Matt, "Matt, is there anything I can get you." YOUNG MATT tells Matt's Mom, "Can I have a dog with mustard and a diet coke?" MATT'S MOM tells Young Matt, "Coming right up." Matt's Mom is about to leave until Young Matt watches Derek Jeter warming up on the field. Matt's Mom goes over to Matt and talk to them. MATT'S MOM tells Young Matt, "This is your dream is it?" YOUNG MATT tells Matt's Mom, "Derek Jeter look so free out there and happy. Playing in that field, like magic. I want that someday. Someday that will be me up their playing in the A.L. Championship like him." MATT'S MOM tells Young Matt, "I'm sure you will Matt." YOUNG MATT tells Matt's Mom, "I want to play in that stadium someday. You think I can do it." MATT'S MOM tells Young Matt, "Listen Matt, anything you want in life. Go get it, don't hold yourself back. You go out their fight to get it. Anything you want, if you work for it and play your cards anything possible." YOUNG MATT tells Matt's Mom, "You think so, Mom." MATT'S MOM tells Young Matt, "I know so. Do me a favor, don't ever give up on the dream. Because the dream won't give up on you. Wherever you are, I'm right their besides you on right here and right now." Young Matt hugs his mother. YOUNG MATT tells his Mom, "I love you Mom." MATT'S MOM tells Young Matt, "I love you too Mom." Matt looks onto the baseball field for a minute where the Yankees are practicing. Matt stops by the Boston Cemetery to visit his Mom's grave. Matt is a little teary and Matt is carrying something for her Mother. His Yankees Jersey and his ball cap for his mother's grave. MATT tells himself, "I actually did it Mom. Thank you, for not giving up. I got something for you." Matt puts his Yankees Jersey and his ball cap on her grave for a minute. MATT tells himself, "I told you I could do it. Not bad from a kid from Boston." Barbara enters Reynold's Office and carrying information that he wanted about this team. REYNOLDS tells Barbara, "Well Barbara, what did you find out?" BARBARA tells Reynolds, "Well, I got some bad news, good news, bad news and more good news. How you want to go first Mr. Reynolds?" REYNOLDS tells Barbara, "Just tell me did you find anything about this team. Use of steroids, cork bats or gambling." BARBARA tells Reynolds, "The bad news I checked it out. We got nothing on them using steroids, gambling or cork bats." REYNOLDS tells Barbara, "Nothing." BARBARA tells Reynolds, "Not even a couple of DUI's or knocking up a girl. The DUI or knocking up a girl is small time stuff. But if it was steroids, cork bats or gambling, it would've made them forfeit the championship or remove the players off the team." REYNOLDS tells Barbara, "So, what's the good news?" BARBARA tells Reynolds, "One of the players of that team. Is not exactly who they thought they are? One of them is an imposter or a gate crasher." Barbara gives the file about Matt to Reynolds and Reynolds grabs it and observes it for a minute. REYNOLDS tells Barbara, "Who is that imposter anyway?" BARBARA tells Reynolds, "Matt Schultz, he was never invited to camp or was on the list. I made a check with the Phillies farm them, they never heard of Matt. They only heard of Axel Schultz, the one who was supposed to be invited to camp not Matt." REYNOLDS tells Barbara, "Are you saying Schultz was invited here buy accident and he was impersonating a player of this team. This day is getting better, so let's find this Axel Schultz guy, he can help us expose him and we can call Ryan and baseball commissioner to deal with our impostor." BARBARA tells Reynolds, "You remember the more bad news I told you about." REYNOLDS tells Barbara, "What is it?" BARBARA tells Reynolds, "Axel is dead, he died in a car crash coming to spring training. He was driving and he got sideswiped and crashed. He died by injuries and there was a funeral about a few weeks ago during spring training. So, I don't think he can help us." REYNOLDS tells Barbara, "Great, now what we can deal. We need a smear campaign to get rid of him and get this team to lose the pennant." BARBARA tells Reynolds, "There is more good news and what we call final news." REYNOLDS tells Barbara, "What did you got?" BARBARA tells Reynolds. "We don't need Axel to expose. We have all the info on Schultz ourselves. We can tip off the press and the tabloids about our imposter. Once the baseball commissioner and Green see this. They'll have no choice to kick him off the team and ban him from baseball." REYNOLDS tells Barbara, "Or have him arrested for impersonating a baseball player. Barbara make the call to New York Times. It's time we give them a tip about our little friend here." BARBARA tells Reynolds, "You know sir, why don't you do the honors." REYNOLDS tells Barbara, "I'll be happy too." Reynolds picks up the phone and makes a call to New York Times. REYNOLDS talks on the phone, "Hello, get me Jack Truman for Sports Editing. Hello Jack, listen I need a favor. Trust me, I have a topic for you." Matt is sitting down in his front desk in the first floor and signing autographs for a twelve year old kid. MATT tells Jordan, "Here you go, Jordan." Matt finishes signing his autograph to Jordan and gives it to him. Jordan grabs his autograph from Matt and observes it for a minute. JORDAN tells Matt, "Thanks Matt." MATT tells Jordan, "Listen, not a word. I don't even know why I'm here. I don't want it to be a media frenzy here." JORDAN tells Matt, "No problemo, Matt. Thanks for the autograph." MATT tells Jordan, "Sure thing, I'll see you in the Al Championship." JORDAN tells Matt, "Bye Matt!" MATT tells Jordan, "See ya, kid." Jordan leaves and Ashley goes over to Matt and talk to him. ASHLEY tells Matt, "Hey honey." MATT tells Ashley, "Hey baby." Matt and Ashley makes out with Ashley for a minute and stops. ASHLEY tells Matt, "So, when do you get off?" MATT tells Ashley, "Just for a couple of minutes. I have that Nike photo shoot with your dad after I get off."

ASHLEY tells Matt, "What about lunch, I thought we were going to have lunch when you get off work." MATT tells Ashley, "Riley, called me a last minute. The Nike Photo Shoot is happening today. So, I have to go. Don't worry, it won't take long. It's going to take us an hour to finish the shoot and then will go to lunch." ASHLEY tells Matt, "I love it when you compromise." MATT tells Ashley, "Don't I know it?" Riley enters the library and carrying a paper of New York Times. He looks really mad for a minute. MATT tells Riley, "Hey Riley, what are you doing here? I thought we were going to meet at shoot in a few minutes." RILEY tells Matt, "We don't have to worry about the photo shoot. Because Luigi already cancelled it." MATT tells Riley, "Wait a minute, your agent cancelled our Nike photo shoot." RILEY tells Matt, "There is a photo shoot for me, but not you. You're off the cover." MATT tells Riley, "I don't get it, what's going on." RILEY tells Matt, "Maybe you can explain this. I just got the paper yesterday in my house and read a front page article about you." Riley puts the New York Times paper down on the table and Riley grabs it and observes it for a minute. Riley reads this, it doesn't look good. Yankees fake player that's on the front page. RILEY tells Matt, "What's your name again, Axel, Matt. I don't know, how about asshole does it." MATT tells Riley, "I don't know how this happened." RILEY tells Matt, "One thing, I know. Just tell me this is not true. That you're not a impostor, who impersonating a player that was invited to camp." ASHLEY tells Matt, "Yeah, Matt tell me it's not true." Riley looks at them for a minute and starts explaining. MATT tells them, "It's true, Axel Schultz was supposed to be invited to camp not me." Ashley slaps Matt in the face for a minute. ASHLEY tells Matt, "I had a boyfriend who cheated on me, when I visited him in Yale. I'm not going through that again." MATT tells Ashley, "I thought you and Lucas broke up, because of the commute." ASHLEY tells Matt, "I wanted to save face. So, no one doesn't feel sorry for me. He cheated on me with a sorority girl when I visited him to the dorm. You know, pretending to be somebody else is a lot worse than Lucas cheating on me." RILEY tells Matt, "I don't even know who you are anymore. Leave us alone." Riley and Ashley are upset for a minute, Matt exits the front desk and stops them from leaving. MATT tells Riley, "Look guys, I'm really sorry I lied about who I am. I knew sooner or later, somebody would find out about me. I guess somebody did." RILEY tells Matt, "You know what, I don't even care. You can tell it to Jeff and Mr. Jackson the GM. I sure he and the owner Mr. Green wants to speak to you tomorrow. That's the reason why he wanted to call me. Don't do us any favors." MATT tells them, "Look guys, just give me a second than you can leave." ASHLEY tells Matt, "You got one second, tell me you were drafted by the Philadelphia Phillies and played for the Clearwater Threshers, the Philadelphia Phillies farm team you played for the last six years. You were a shortstop for that team and not really that good. You haven't got a hit for the last six years. It's one of the main reasons, you weren't called up or is that a lie too." MATT tells Ashley, "No, that wasn't me. It was Axel. Axel Schultz, the one who was supposed to be invited to Spring Training, not me." ASHLEY tells Matt, "So tell me, Matt who are you. Why did you lie to us who you are?" MATT tells Riley, "My name is Matt Schultz, I'm from Boston Massachusetts. I was a college star in my baseball team in Fresno State where I took my team to the College World Series. Got selected to play in the Cape League after my team won the series. I played for Harwich Mariners and took his team to a cape league championship. I hit a inside the park home run than won the championship and blew my knee out that cost me a shot in the majors. My career in baseball was over, so I went back to college finish up my degree and took intern job here. The rest is history." RILEY tells Matt, "So tell us about how you lied your way to spring training." MATT tells Riley, "I'm getting to it. My friend Gary who works as a bartender in the Red Sky Bar got tickets for Spring Training for me and my other pal Rick to watch a couple of games in Florida. Right after we landed in the hotel, Rick and Gary wanted go to Spring Break in Daytona, Right after they check in the hotel. I declined, I went to the Stadium to check it out before I go back to the hotel for the game tomorrow. I saw Jeff, he thought I was Axel Schultz that was invited here, he let me in. I thought I was invited here by a contest buy being a millionth customer to work out with the team. I met you and the rest of the team, I found out by Jeff that I was actually trying out for the team and I got in here by accident." ASHLEY tells Matt, "So, you're saying you went there by accident. Why didn't you just tell anybody?" MATT tells Riley, "At first, when I found out that I was trying out for the team. I was going to tell Jeff the truth and he would've let me leave. Or the real Axel would expose me, I would've gotten a lot of trouble. But, I wanted to be there. This was my second chance to play in the majors. It felt great to be back in the game. Like I did in the cape leagues. At least I wanted one moment, to be on top. I did." RILEY tells Matt, "I guess I understand, I would've done the same thing you did if it was me. You were desperate and you wanted to know what it felt like to chase your dream for one day. Trust me, it wasn't easy staying in the minors for two years." MATT tells Riley, "So, does that mean you forgive me?" RILEY tells Matt, "Not yet". Riley punches Matt in the face lightly for a minute. RILEY tells Matt, "Now I forgive you." MATT tells Ashley, "What about you Ashley?" ASHLEY tells Matt, "I don't know, I just don't know how to pencil this in right now, Just give me some time. I'm sorry, I just need to be alone right now." Ashley leaves and she's totally upset about this situation. Matt was about to go after her for a minute and Riley stops him for a minute. RILEY tells Matt, "Just give her some time man, she's need to pencil everything before she forgives you." MATT tells Riley, "I don't know, how that will be. What's going too happened?" RILEY tells Matt, "Tomorrow, you have to go see Jeff. He'll take you to see Mr. Green." MATT tells Riley, "The owner of the club." RILEY tells Matt, "Yeah, and he's figure out what he's going to do to you." MATT tells Riley, "The way you look, it's not good." RILEY tells Matt, "Don't worry, if you need anybody to defend you, it'll be me. I have your back." MATT tells Riley, "Thanks Riley." RILEY tells Matt, "Hey, no problemo." Ryan is sitting down in chair and George and Jeff are standing up listening to Matt side of the story with Riley defending him in Ryan's Office. Matt and Riley are sitting down in their chairs explaining Matt's side of the story to Ryan. RYAN tells them, "You know Mr. Schultz from reading the headlines in the New York Times about this incident. I wanted to hear from you, if any of these rumors are true. That you impersonating a dead player that was supposed to be invited to camp in Spring Training." MATT tells George, "Yes sir, it's true. But not the way you thought it happened." GEORGE tells Riley, "Is there anyone who could back you up in this story Schuttz." RILEY tells George, "Well, I did. Look, Mr. Sanders, Mr. Schultz I know what Mr. Schultz did is wrong, but his heart is in the right place." GEORGE tells Matt, "Mr. Riley, why are you here." RILEY tells George, "I'm here to testify on Mr. Schultz behalf." GEORGE tells Riley, "This is not a trial Riley. But it will be if we file charges to the DA on Mr. Schultz incident that would give him jail time. You're looking at a few years, Schultz. Is there anything you want to say, to defend yourself." RILEY tells them, "He won't, but I will. One thing first what about the Baseball Commissioner, what does he say about this incident." GEORGE tells them, "Commissioner said, we could handle it from here. It will be our call, about this situation." RILEY tells Jeff, "Okay, but I like to say something on my teammate's defense if it's okay with you guys." JEFF tells Riley, "Go ahead, Riley." RILEY tells them, "We've been in a losing streak for two years. This club been falling apart for a long time, but we been through it all. The depression, the steroid scandal, the black sox series and this. We always found a way to overcome it. I know you guys are thinking about banning my friend from this league and Baseball League. I don't think you should, Mr. Green took a chance on all of us. Of all the players and managers he would've picked, he picked us. We weren't exactly team that would ever win the pennant, but we did and were one game in the pennant. I know you guys would love go by the book and kick him out or charge him for anything. But you're wrong, you do that to him. You're doing that to all of us. One of us had lied to get in here, but he had a reason. He wanted to live out his dream to play here just once. He may did it the wrong way, but if he had do it over again. He would've done the same thing. So would I, that's the reason why you picked us. You took a chance on us. Just like Matt had to lie his way in to be part of the team. For the entire season, he was part of the team and the glue kept this team together. He was also the guy who made us believe what The Runaway Boys stood for. And it stood for, we fight for the American dream for all mankind to believe in freedom. Isn't that how our forefathers got here. So, I think you ban him from this league or this team. Or charge him for anything. It's your call." GEORGE tells Riley, "Well, it's an amazing speech Riley. I loved it, but the most important fact Mr. Schultz. That you impersonated a dead player arriving in spring training. Not only should I ban you from this team or this league. I should press charges. We're calling the DA, guys take Mr. Schultz in the holding cell before the police arrive." RILEY tells Jeff, "Wait, Mr. Sanders it's a little uncalled for." JEFF tells Matt, "Yeah, me too." MATT tells Ryan, "Look guys, I'm really sorry. Please, I'll do anything. Please!" RYAN tells Matt, "Relax guys, I'm not pressing charges on Schultz. But, I will give you a choice Mr. Schultz." MATT tells Ryan, "What are the choices?" RYAN tells Matt, "You can call a press conference in the afternoon and explain about how you got here and you can stay in the team and if you do get this team to the pennant. You have a five year 10 million dollar contract with this team, you can keep your endorsements make a public apology to Axel Schultz and his family." MATT tells Ryan, "What's the second choice? " RYAN tells Matt, "The same, but you will resign from this team and apology to New York. The choice is up to you." MATT tells George, "You were never going to press charges to the DA or ban me from the league. This was a test wasn't it?" GEORGE tells Jeff, "You betcha, I knew I smell a smear campaign when I saw it. I knew the person who wanted this team so badly, he would've done anything to get this team." JEFF tells them, "And weren't going to lose out our two star players from this jerk." RILEY tells Ryan, "So who was this asshole that tried to take over this team and tried to smear me?" RYAN tells Matt, "The same asshole were going to face in the final championship game and we have a lot of work to do. Matt go make that press conference." MATT tells Ryan, "Yes sir." RYAN tells Matt, "Remember, it's your choice. Whatever you decide the team has your back and you're always welcome here anytime you want." Matt is a little teary. MATT tells Ryan, "I know what to say." ESPN, FOX Sports, FOX and CNN journalist are listening to Matt on the podium in the press conference room and where Riley is sitting down in his chair next to the podium with Jeff, Ryan, George and Reynolds. Ashley, Jessica, Roger, David, Gary and Rick are sitting down with the reporters listening to Matt's statement about the incident. MATT tells them, "That's how I got here. It was stupidest thing I ever did. I like to give out a condolence to Axel and his family. The Yankees will dedicate this game for him and name a scholarship after him. The truth is, I living out Axel's dream. I know it was fate he wanted me to fill in his shoes and take this team all the way. I knew he wanted me to be here and so did I. It may been misunderstanding, I would never change anything. I'll be happy take some questions right now." ESPN reporter gets up from his chair and ask Matt a question. ESPN REPORTER tells Matt, "Matt, Nick Vexel ESPN. So, is true you impersonated this Axel Schultz?" MATT tells the reporter, "Yes!" NICK tells Matt, "But why?" MATT tells them, "I guess I was trying to live out a dream. When I knew my baseball career was over in the Cape League Championship when I blew my knee out in the inside the park home run. I felt like I was lost somewhere. When I found out I was accidentally invited to spring training and I figured out it wasn't me that was being invited. It was somebody else." NICK tells Matt, "So, why didn't you just tell Linwood or anybody else about this misunderstanding?" MATT tells them, "I thought about it, if I did. They just let me leave or maybe this was my second chance reliving my dream to Baseball League. My Mom and I used to Yankees fans, I always told her that someday I would played in the same field with greatest players in that league. I did, were reliving that dream. At first, I was scared, that somebody would expose me for impersonating Axel. But I didn't care, this was the first time I get to live out my dream and I was living out Axel's too. Like I said, he wanted me to be here just like I did." NICK tells Matt, "So, why now. Who was trying to expose you?" MATT tells them, "It was somebody who wasn't exactly a Yankees fan. He would've found dirt on anyone or try to smear me. So, I can be kicked out and this team would lose." NICK tells Matt,

"Any idea, who made this smear campaign on you and this team?" MATT tells them, "Yeah, I did. But, I'm not going to give out a name. Because if I did, I'll be bad as him. One thing I will do finish what I started." NICK tells them, "What's that?" MATT tells them, "I spoke to Ryan Green the owner of this team and my manager Jeff Linwood. I have a choice, I call this press conference to give out an apology to everybody in New York and all the baseball fans of the world. Especially to my team and I would resign. But I'm still welcome here to be here as a fan." NICK tells them, "What was the second choice?" MATT tells them, "The same and I don't resign. I finish out my season and if I help them win the pennant. I can stay here permanently." NICK tells Matt, "So, what's the choice?" MATT tells Jeff, "So, I only got one choice. I'm not going anywhere if that's okay with Skipper." Riley gets up from his seat and goes to the podium and say something. RILEY tells them, "Before Jeff makes his decision. I got one thing to say, whatever Jeff or Ryan decision. I have one decision to say, I'm not going to play for anybody but Matt Schultz I believe in him. He's the main reason, I came back from the dead. I was so lost for two years, he helped me found my way back. He's the heart of the team, Me and Riley were the M&M Men. It's your choice guys." David gets up from his chair and say something to Jeff. DAVID tells them, "That goes for me too." Roger, Gary, Rick, Ashley, Jessica and all the Yankee Players get up from their chairs to cheer on Matt. Ryan, George and Jeff get up from their chair to support Matt. Reynolds doesn't support him. Jeff goes over to the podium and say something. JEFF tells the reporters, "Matthew Schultz is our number one shortstop of the The Runaway Boys. He's going to stay as the The Runaway Boys. We have an American League Championship to win, we can't do without number one shortstop and our star pitcher the M&M guys. We have a lot of work to do. Let's do it." Everybody starts cheering for a minute and Reynolds doesn't applaud. REYNOLDS tells himself, "It doesn't matter now, the team will be mine when they choke tomorrow night." Everybody starts changing in their uniforms, Riley goes over to Matt talk to him in the Yankees Locker Room in Yankees Stadium. RILEY tells Matt, "You okay, man." MATT tells Riley, "Hey, I'm fine. I waited my whole life for this. I just wish…?" Riley interrupts Matt for a minute. RILEY tells Matt, "Ashley will be here." MATT tells Riley, "How do you know?" RILEY tells Matt, "Trust me." Riley exit's the locker and heads to the vending machine. David and Roger goes over to Matt and talk to them. MATT tells them, "Hey guys." ROGER tells Matt, "Hey Matt. I just wanted to say thank you, for talking to our dads and getting them to come." DAVID tells Matt, "First time, me and my dad speak the same language. Without some ordung shit. I think he and our family are going to be more liberal from now on." MATT tells David, "How liberal?" DAVID tells Matt, "I think he can use a little modern conveniences from now on. He doesn't care about what the bishop or the elders think. He wanted to do it for a long time. Now he does and were going to have equal rights for everybody from now on." ROGER tells Matt, "Me and my dad are doing the same thing. Having equal rights for both of us, he even got a Yankees ball cap and shirt to root for me and my team." MATT tells them, "Thanks guys." ROGER tells Matt, "Hey, no problemo. See you in the dugout." Roger and David exits the locker room and head to the dugout. Ashley enters the dugout and goes over talk to Matt. Ashley makes out with Matt for a minute and stops. MATT tells Ashley, "What's that for?" ASHLEY tells Matt, "I lied about my resume about having full experience working in my library in high school. I hanged out a lot there, I never had a lot of experience working in one. Somewhere, I always wanted to work at one and I wanted to be a writer their too someday. Being a head librarian, writing a top novel and having it New York Times best seller. I guess I kind of lied my way in to live out a dream" MATT tells Ashley, "I guess were both liars, but about being head librarian. Our boss has his book published, he's going to be writing full time. So, he quit and left me the place. So, I thought why not you take over while I'm playing next season." ASHLEY tells Matt, "You're playing next season." MATT tells Ashley, "If I win this championship I could you never know. I could always use a deputy head librarian." ASHLEY tells Matt, "I think you have yourself a deputy." MATT tells Ashley, "I like to have that in writing." Matt and Ashley starts making out for a minute. A lot of people are entering the stadium, their sitting down in al championship game of the world and buying t-shirts and ball caps of The Runaway Boys on it in Yankees Stadium. RAY'S VOICE tells the fans, "Welcome Fans to Yankees Stadium and where we have a sellout crowd with 50,000 thousand Yanks who are here with the final game of the AL championship." Ray and Al are broadcasting Al Championship game and they're having a hot dog and a bottle of miller lite in the Broadcasting booth. AL tells the fans, "It's a chance for the Yanks to have another shot of World Series against the number one team Texas Rangers." RAY tells the fans, "The Texas Rangers star player and Riley's number one rival Rick Lavene. Remember whoever the wins the pennant will go to the World Series." AL tells the fans, "And the loser will go home and will be the end of the season for them. I always wanted to say that." AL'S VOICE tells the fans, "And remember this is for all the marbles, the whole enchilada. The winner will win the pennant and go to the World Series. The loser will go home and this season will be over." Where the Texas Rangers are hearing Ray's Voice on the radio in their dugout. Ryan, George and Reynolds are in the Owners box and sitting down watching the final game. Jeff is giving out a speech to his teammates and motivating them too in the Yankees Dugout. JEFF tells them, "I'm proud of you guys. We come a long way. Win or lose, I'm proud of you guys. I believe in all of you. Let's not win this for New York, let's this win for all of us. Especially all the fans that came out here and believed us. Let's do it for them and for us all. It's time we bring back that AL championship back where it belongs. To us!" MATT tells them, "You heard him, let's do it." RILEY tells them, "Let's do it! Come on!" The The Runaway Boys head to the baseball field. The Yankees announcer calls them out. THE RUNAWAY BOYS ANNOUNCER tells the fans, "Ladies and Gentleman, you're The Runaway Boys!" Everybody starts cheering for them in the baseball field. AL'S VOICE tells the fans, "Starting pitcher of this game Mike Riley. 16 and 9 of this season and ERA 2.12 with 300 strike outs." RAY'S VOICE tells the fans, "Whatever happens in this game this was a tremendous comeback for Mike Riley." Riley is on the mound and sees Rangers batter on home plate. RAY'S VOICE tells the fans, "It's top of the first, Riley makes the pitch." Riley throws the ball hard, Rangers batter swings his bat and misses. The scoreboard says strike one. Riley throws the ball hard, Rangers batter swings his bat again and misses. Riley throws another ball hard, Rangers batter swings again and misses. HOME PLATE UMPIRE tells the batter, "Strike, you're out!" Everybody is cheering, Riley throws the ball to the next batter and Rangers batter swings his bat and misses. HOME PLATE UMPIRE tells the batter, "Strike, you're out." AL'S VOICE tells the fans, "How about that, three strikes and Riley retires the side." Roger is up to bat and ready for the pitch. RAY'S VOICE tells the fans, "Bottom of the second, Punjaab is ready to bat." Roger sees his father wearing Yankees t-shirt and his mother and his two sisters routing for him. ROGER'S FATHER cheers for his son, "Come on, son. You can do it." Ranger's pitcher throws the ball hard, Roger swings his bat and hits it near left field and it's a pop up fly where Ranger's left fielder catches it. RAY'S VOICE tells the fans "Dawson makes the pitch, Punjaab hits it to left field for a pop up fly where that's end the second inning." Riley is on the mound, throws the ball hard and Rangers batters swings his bat and misses it. HOME PLATE UMPIRE tells the batter, "Strike, you're out!" Riley throws the ball hard, the next Rangers batter swings his bat and misses it. HOME PLATE UMPIRE tells the batter, "Strike, you're out!" Riley throws the ball hard, the next Rangers batter swings his bat and misses it. HOME PLATE UMPIRE tells the batter, "Strike, you're out!" Riley throws the ball hard, the next Rangers batter swings his bat and misses it. HOME PLATE UMPIRE tells the batter, "Strike, you're out!" Riley throws the ball hard, the next Rangers batter swings his bat and hits it near second and third base. AL'S VOICE tells the fans, "Riley makes a throw, Lennberry got a piece of it. Hits it near left field." Lennberry hit's the ball near second and third and Matt dives in and catches the ball and throws the ball at third base and tag out the next Texas Ranger's batter. THIRD BASE UMPIRE tells them, "You're out!" RAY'S VOICE tells the fans, "Schultz, caught it and throws the ball at third and retires the fifth inning." Matt is up to bat at home plate and David is on third base. Dawson is on the mound and ready to pitch. AL'S VOICE tells the fans, "Bottom of the fifth, Yoder is on third and Schultz is up to bat. Dawson makes the pitch." Dawson throws the ball hard, Matt sees right field and Matt swings his bat and hits it near the right field wall. Matt hit's the ball and hits near the right field wall, Matt runs up to third base and David runs all the way to home plate. The ball hit's the right field wall and falls down on the grass. The Rangers right fielder grabs the ball on the grass and throws it to third. RAY'S VOICE tells the fans, "Schultz hits it near right field wall and Leon grabs the ball from the green and throws it to third while Yoder makes it to home." Leon throws the ball at third, the Rangers third baseman caught the ball and tries to tag out Matt. But misses him, when Matt slides to third safe and sound and third base umpire makes the call. THIRD BASE UMPIRE tells Matt, "Safe!" AL'S VOICE tells the fans, "Riley is safe at third and Yoder makes the score. That gives the Yanks 1 to nothing lead." Ryan, George and Reynolds are watching the game in the Owner's Box. Reynolds is not really pleased about this game where everybody is cheering. REYNOLDS tells George, "Please, it was just one lucky run. They're not going to win it." GEORGE tells Reynolds, "You never know, it's only the fifth inning. They could win this, Reynolds." REYNOLDS tells George, "Yeah, right. George Lucas can win an Oscar.

Don't make me laugh. You'll be signing this team to me, when they lose." RYAN tells Reynolds, "The game is not over yet Reynolds. And by the way, next try." REYNOLDS tells them, "I don't know what you're talking about?" GEORGE tells Reynolds, "We know you're the one who tip off the press about Schultz. So, we can throw him out of the game and find out some dirt on us. So that way we forfeit the championship to the Rangers and sign the company." RYAN tells Reynolds, "Or lose out our favorite player, so the Yanks will lose." REYNOLDS tells Ryan, "That's a very serious accusation. You have nothing to back it up." RYAN tells Reynolds, "No, we don't. But we know it was you the whole time." REYNOLDS tells Ryan, "You have nothing on me, the team is still going to lose out to me and my favorite team. You'll see." Riley is on the mound and throws the ball hard in the baseball field. The Ranger's batter swings his bat and misses. HOME PLATE UMPIRE tells the batter, "Strike, you're out!" Ranger's batter exit's the home plate and goes back to the dugout. The next Rangers batter comes to home plate and ready to bat. Riley throws the ball hard and the Rangers batter swings his bat and hits it near the centerfield wall. RAY'S VOICE tells the fans, "Riley makes the throw Laville hits it through the centerfield wall." David sees the ball going over to the centerfield wall, Riley runs fast as he can to centerfield wall, leaps up and catches the ball. AL'S VOICE tells the fans, "Yoder got a jump it and caught it, with an amazing catch that retires the side. Keeps the Yanks leads 1-0 top of the sixth." David's father and his amish family are watching near the Yankees dugout box. DAVID'S FATHER tells David, "That's my son. That's my son out their!" Dawson throws the ball hard, Roger swings his bat and misses it. RAY'S VOICE tells the fans, "Bottom of the sixth, Punjaab swings and strikes out. That's the end of the sixth inning." Riley is on the mound and sees the Rangers batter. Riley throws the ball hard, Rangers batter swings his bat and misses it. HOME PLATE UMPIRE tells the batter, "Strike, you're out!" RAY'S VOICE tells the fans, "Riley throws and Hanks swings and gets stuck out." Hanks leaves the home plate and Lavene is up to bat. HOME PLATE UMPIRE tells the fans, "Top of the eighth two batters are on second and third. Looks whose up to bat." THE RUNAWAY BOYS ANNOUNCER tells the fans, "Number 25 first baseman Rick Lavene." Lavene is up on home plate and read to bat. LAVENE tells Riley, "I have to hand it to you, Riley. I didn't know you were going to make it this far." RILEY tells Lavene, "Only if we win." LAVENE tells Riley, "Don't count your day job, Riley. I always win, you're always going to be a loser. Enjoy another season in the minor's dickface." RILEY tells himself, "We'll see about that." Riley throws the ball hard, Lavene swings his bat and hits it out of the park. AL'S VOICE tells the fans, "Riley throws, Lavene hit's it out of the park. The Rangers are up to 3-1 in top of the eighth." Everybody starts booing for a minute. Ryan, George and Reynolds are watching the game in the owner's box. Reynolds is really pleased about this game. REYNOLDS tells them, "That will shut these out of shape losers up. I love Reynolds, he is my hero. I wondered if he would love to invest in my land development deal. I think you boys better grab out your pen, this team is mine." GEORGE tells Reynolds, "The game is not over yet, Reynolds. It's only the eighth inning." REYNOLDS tells them, "Forget it, that team already chocked. The Rangers and the Yanks are 3-3 in the series. Looks the Rangers are going to win it all. So much for your star player who already chocked in the last inning just like he did two years ago." RYAN tells Reynolds, "Like I said, Reynolds game is not over yet." REYNOLDS tells Ryan, "Not while I'm sitting. One more inning this team is mine." Ryan is already praying for a miracle. RYAN tells Reynolds, "Well see about that. Come on, guys. You can do it, please do it for the team and for us please god give us a miracle, please I'm begging you!" Roger is on home plate and up to bat and Dawson is on the mound in the baseball field. RAY'S VOICE tells the fans, "It's bottom of the eight and two outs. Punjaab is up to bat. His batting average is up 370, 120 rbi's and 52 homers." AL'S VOICE tells the fans, "We need a miracle to win." Dawson throws the ball hard, Roger swings his bat and hit's the ball right out of the park the centerfield wall. RAY'S VOICE tells the fans, "Dawson's makes the pitch and Punjaab hits it right out of the center field wall. And it's out of there." Everybody starts cheering and Roger runs to the four bases. RAY'S VOICE tells the fans, "The score is up to 3-2, the Yanks are two runs behind." Jeff sees David sitting down on the bench and tells him he's up in the Dugout. JEFF tells Yoder, "Yoder, you're up!" Yoder is about to get up from the bench and sees Matt going over talk to Jeff. MATT tells Jeff, "Jeff, before we send Yoder up to bat. I have an idea to get to the lead." JEFF tells Matt, "What is it?" MATT tells Jeff, "Let Yoder, get hit by a pitch and let me pinch hit." JEFF tells Matt, "Well Matt, we don't need three bases. We need a home run to win." MATT tells Jeff, "I know that, so I going to use the same hit I use to win the championship game in Cape League." JEFF tells Matt, "You mean the hit that blew out your knee that cost you a shot in the majors." MATT tells Jeff, "That's the one." JEFF tells Matt, "I don't know Matt it's too risky." MATT tells Jeff, "I know, but I already perfected it. I know I can do it, I been practicing it really hard. I'll never know if I can do it. If I don't take a chance on it." JEFF tells David, "Okay, get ready. David, listen I need a favor." David is up to home plate and ready to bat and Dawson is on the mound in the baseball field. David sees the signal from Jeff. RAY'S VOICE tells the fans, "The Yanks are two runs behind, they need a miracle to win. Dawson is on the mound and Yoder is up to bat. His batting average is up to 320 and 120 rbi's, let's see what he can do." Dawson throws the ball hard, David tries to lean a little on home plate. The ball hits David on the back and it's hit by a pitch. AL'S VOICE tells the fans, "Dawson throws it and hits Yoder on the back. He's gets hit by a pitch and the tying run is on first." HOME PLATE UMPIRE tells the player, "Hit by a pitch, take your base." The crowd boos and Yoder takes his base at first. Matt is up to bat and heads to home plate. RAY'S VOICE tells the fans, "This is a Cinderella story. Matt Schultz, the head librarian of the New York Public Library, who used to stamp out books is now stamping out inside the park home runs." AL'S VOICE tells the fans, "This guy was a college World Series star, blew his knee out winning the championship game in the Cape League. Stamping out book for a couple of years and came out of nowhere and turn this team around." RAY'S VOICE tells the fans, "That's right, Al. His batting average 352, 45 inside the park home runs and 600 runs for this season. Now, can this Cinderella Man turns this game around or he can kiss his Cinderella season goodbye. Were about to find out." Dawson throws the ball hard, Matt swings his bat and hit's the left field foul line. RAY'S VOICE tells the fans, "Dawson makes the pitch, Schultz swings it left field. But it's foul." Dawson throws the ball hard again, Matt swings his bat and misses it. HOME PLATE UMPIRE calls the play, "Strike two!" Everybody is chanting M&M and sees cardboard cut outs of Matt and Riley calling them M&M! YANKEES FANS tells the fans, "M&M, M&M, M&M!" Ashley is sitting next to Julie, Rick and Gary near the dugout box. ASHLEY tells Riley, "Come on, Matt! I know you can do it! I believe in you,

M&M Man!" JULIE, RICK AND GARY tells Riley, "M&M, M&M, M&M!" Matt smiles a little for a minute and has an idea. MATT tells the fans, "For you Mom!" Matt points out to the sky to Dawson and he knows what to expect. AL'S VOICE tells the fans, "Schultz is pointing out to sky. Looks like he's going to hit infield fly homerun. Nobody ever hit the infield fly homerun except Babe Ruth when he went against the Sox in the twenties. Schultz hit's the infield fly in the championship game in the Cape Leagues that will won him the game a couple of years ago. Looks like history is going to repeat itself." Dawson is ready to make the pitch after his warm up. RAY'S VOICE tells the fans, "Dawson's finish his warm up and now he's ready." Dawson throws the ball hard, Matt swings his bat and hit's it near the centerfield wall. AL'S VOICE tells the fans, "Dawson throws, Matt swings and hit's through the centerfield wall. That will make it three bases and the Yanks will tie the game." The ball hit's the centerfield wall and the ball falls down on the grass. David and Matt starts running through four bases. Rangers centerfielder grabs the ball and throws it to fourth base. David makes it home and Matt is going for the lead of the game and running to fourth base. RAY'S VOICE tells the fans, "Chef grab the ball and throws it to home. Yoder scores and it looks Schultz is going for home and for the lead." The Rangers catcher caught the ball and Matt slides through fourth base. The Rangers catcher tries to tag out Matt, but Matt makes it home safe and sound. AL'S VOICE tells the fans, "Schultz slides through and...?" The home plate umpire makes the call. HOME PLATE UMPIRE tells the players, "Safe! Safe!" RAY'S VOICE tells the fans, "The Yanks are up to 4-3. For Matt's inside the park home run. That record is going to be in history books years to come." Ryan, George and Reynolds are watching the game in the owner's box. Reynolds is not pleased with the results. REYNOLDS tells them, "Don't worry, Riley is going to choke on the ninth. Trust me, he will. This team will be mine, when Riley chokes. I know so." Jeff sees Riley and gives him a pep talk in the Yankees Dugout. JEFF tells his son, "Hey Riley, one more inning and we win the whole thing. Whatever happens, I believe in you." RILEY tells Jeff, "Thanks Skipper." JEFF tells Riley, "Let's finish this thing." RILEY tells Jeff, "You got it." Back in the baseball field. The Yankees team is ready to get out there on the field, Riley doesn't see the bat and trips over the bat and hits his pitching arm. A lot of people are stunned and so is Jeff. Matt goes over to Riley to see if he's okay. JEFF tells his son, "Riley, you okay." MATT tells Riley, "Riley, how many fingers I'm holding up." Matt puts three fingers up. RILEY tells Matt, "Two!" MATT tells Riley, "He's fine." Riley gets up from the grass and heads to the mound. Everybody is cheering for Riley. Riley sees the baseball, grabs it and sees his catcher and throws the ball to the catcher and the catcher misses it. YANKEES CATCHER ask Riley, "Riley, you okay. What's going on?" RILEY tells himself, "Oh man, my pitching arm it's gone." Ryan, George and Reynolds are watching the game in the Owner's Box. Reynolds is pleased with the results. REYNOLDS tells them, "I told you Riley, chocked. Looks like the team is mine. Signed and sealed to me." Ryan and George are upset about this. RYAN tells George, "We need a miracle." GEORGE tells Ryan, "I know!" Riley is up on the mound and tells his catcher something in the baseball field. RILEY calls the team, "Time!" RAY'S VOICE tells the fans, "Yankees are calling for a time out!" Riley, David and Roger goes over to the mound talk to Riley. RILEY tells them, "My pitching arm is gone. I can't throw it hard anymore." MATT tells them, "What do you want to do?" RILEY tells them, "I'm going to finish this inning. But I need everybody's help. You're with me!" MATT tells them, "Yeah, were in!" ALL OF THEM tells themselves, "Yanks!" Matt, David and Roger are back in their positions and Rangers batter is on home plate. RAY'S VOICE tells the fans, "Conference is over, remember the Yanks need three outs to win the pennant." Riley makes the signal to the catcher and got it. Riley walks the Rangers batter to first. RAY'S VOICE tells the fans, "That's ball four, Alvin takes his base." Yankees catcher throws the ball to Riley and misses the catch and can't find the ball to the mound. AL'S VOICE tells the fans, "Young throws the ball to Riley, but misses it and Riley can't find it on the mound. Alvin steals second." Young never threw the ball to Riley, it was right his behind the catcher's glove. Young throws the ball to second and the Yankees second baseman catches it and tags out Alvin. AL'S VOICE tells the fans, "Young never threw it to Riley, Young throws it to second." SECOND BASE UMPIRE tells the Alvin, "You're out!" AL'S VOICE tells the fans, "Alvin's out! Young never threw the ball to Riley the whole time." The next Rangers batter is up to bat. Riley sees Matt with the signal and Riley throws a slow pitch. Rangers batter sees an easy pitch and Matt alreads dives down on the ground and can't get up for a minute. Rangers batter swings his bat and hits it near second and third base. RAY'S VOICE tells the fans, "Riley makes the slow pitch, Schultz dives down on the dirt too early and Kent hits near left field." Riley rolls over to the right field to third and stops. Yankees second baseman dives down on the dirt near third base and caught the ball. AL'S VOICE tells the fans, "Schultz rolls over the dirt to third and Ventura makes a dive near third and caught the ball that gives the Yanks the second out." Ventura gets up from the dirt and holds the ball where everybody is cheering. RAY'S VOICE tells the fans, "The Yanks are one out from the pennant. Rangers next batter is on home plate and ready to bat. Riley throws the ball slowly and hits Rangers batter in the back." RAY'S VOICE tells the fans, "Riley throws and hits Chaney in the back. The tying run is on first." AL'S VOICE tells the fans, "Guess whose up to bat." Lavene heads to home plate and ready to bat. RILEY tells himself, "Oh god, Lavene." AL'S VOICE tells the fans, "Rick Lavene, last year's MVP, hits 53 homers and 200 rbi's is up to bat. He hit 40 homers over Riley's head." RAY'S VOICE tells the fans, "It's going to take a miracle for Riley to win." Ryan, George and Reynolds are watching the game in the Owner's Box. Reynolds is pleased with the results. REYNOLDS tells them, "Looks like this team, will be mine after all. Hit it out of the park Lavene." Riley is on the mound and Matt goes over talk to him when he calls for time in the baseball field. RILEY tells Matt, "I got us a couple of minutes, I don't know what to do. Lavene is one of the players I can never strike out. I need a miracle to beat him." MATT tells Riley, "You still have the Peanut butter M&M's." RILEY tells Matt, "Even if I eat a couple it won't be enough to strike him out." MATT tells Riley, "Listen to the crows and say to yourself M&M MAN three times." RILEY tells Matt, "What?" MATT tells Riley, "Trust me." Matt goes back to his position for a minute. RAY'S VOICE tells Riley, "Conference is over and Lavene is up to bat. Remember the Yanks are one out from the pennant and the tying run is on first." Matt hears the audience and sees the cut outs of Matt and Riley as the M&M guys. Their chanting. YANKEES FANS cheers for Riley, "M&M, M&M, M&M, M&M!" LAVENE tells Riley, "Let's face it Riley, you're going to choke. You're always going to choke. Enjoy the minors M&M man" RILEY tells himself, "Time to open some can of whoop ass! This is for you baby!" Riley throws the ball hard, Lavene swings his bat and misses. HOME PLATE

UMPIRE tells the fans, "Strike!" Jeff sees the target speed on the radar gun and it's up to 100. Jeff is really happy about that. Riley throws the ball hard again, Lavene swings his bat and misses again. HOME PLATE UMPIRE tells the fans, "Strike!" Jeff sees the speed up to 101. RAY'S VOICE tells the fans, "Riley is 0 and 2 against Lavene." MATT tells Riley, "Strike this bum out." Ryan, George and Reynolds are watching the game in the owner's box. Reynolds isn't pleased with the results. RYAN cheers for Riley and tell him, "Strike the bum out!" REYNOLDS tells Riley, "Choke, Choke, Choke!" Riley sees Lavene on the mound and ready to pitch in the baseball field. LAVENE tells Riley, "Come on, old man. Let's see you can get me out." RILEY tells Lavene, "I don't need to, I just did asshole!" Lavene is a little confused, Riley makes the pitch the ball and throws the ball hard. Lavene swings his bat and misses. HOME PLATE UMPIRE tells Lavene, "Strike, you're out!" Lavene is upset and throws bat on the dirt and kicks it. LAVENE tells himself, "I hate my life, I hate it!" RAY'S VOICE tells the fans, "The Yankees win. The Yankees are going to World Series." Ray and Al get up from their chairs and hug each other in Broadcasting Booth. AL'S VOICE tells the fans, "Yanks Win!" The baseball fans come out of the field and hug the players and David hugs his family and so does Roger in the baseball field. Jeff hugs his wife, Riley hugs Jessica and let go. Riley hugs Matt for a minute. Ryan, George and Reynolds are watching the game in the Owner's Box.

Reynolds isn't pleased with the results. Reynold's get up from his chair and kicks the wall. Ryan and George are happy too. RYAN tells George, "Looks like we win. The team is still mine, you can't tear it down anymore." GEORGE tells Reynolds, "Nice try Reynolds, don't forget our deal. Do you have a pen to sign?" REYNOLDS tells himself, "I hate my life." Reynolds is crying for a minute. Back in field of Yankees Stadium, Riley sees Jessica for a minute on the field and takes out an engagement box with an engagement ring. Jessica starts smiling and hugs Riley and make out with him. Nine months later with a new spring training this season in George M. Steinbrenner Field since Jeff continues on as the new manager. Jeff welcomes a lot of new players for spring training and sees Matt and Riley entering the field. JEFF tells them, "How guys how was your off season." MATT tells Jeff, "It was really amazing, doing that pepsi commercial with Riley, public appearances, the Nike photo shoot and planning our going away trip with Jessica and Ashley." RILEY tells Jeff, "Don't forget about my signing two year deal 25 million dollar contract that will finish my career for the team and your 15 million dollar contract for five year for the club." MATT tells Jeff, "Their waiting for us in the hotel for seating charts after practice for Riley and Jessica's wedding, Ashley is the maid of honor and I'm the best man." RILEY tells Jeff, "So, Dad whose the new rookies." JEFF tells them, "A new pitcher that can't throw and a new shortstop that can't catch either." MATT tells Jeff, "Don't worry, if anyone can shape them up it would be you." JEFF tells Riley, "Not just me, both of us. I can't do it by myself." RILEY tells Jeff, "Don't worry we have your back. Besides if we can made a repeat once and we can do it again. With our help, we can do anything." MATT tells Riley, "I'm in." JEFF tells them, "Me too!" RILEY tells them, "Let's do it!" Matt, Riley and Jeff puts their hands together and shake. MATT, RILEY AND JEFF tells themselves, "M&M!" Matt, Riley and Jeff let go of their hands for a minute. MATT tells them, "Hey, I wondered when the hot dog vendor arrived." RILEY tells Matt, "Yeah, he's in the snack bar." JEFF tells them, "Come on, we don't miss the M&M special." RILEY tells Jeff, "M&M special." JEFF tells Riley, "It was named after you guys." MATT AND RILEY tells Jeff, "Cool! Matt, Riley and Jeff starts laughing and goes inside the baseball field head to the hot dog vendor.

The End.

The End.

ABOUT THE AUTHOR

He is autistic. His family is from India, and he is the first member of his family who was born in America. He graduated in Maryville High School in 1998 and graduated from college at Northwest Missouri State University in 2004. He lived in Los Angeles for three years trying to sell his movie in the big screen. He had an eight-year struggle trying to sell his movie and his book. But he has been rejected for a long time. He wrote this book and dedicates this for his niece, Lakeh Chavala. Sylvester Stallone is his hero, who aspired to be a screenwriter when he took a chance to write Rocky. Bobby wrote twenty movie scripts and three books. This is his first book to be out in the bookstores.